Smoke twisted up from a campfire. By its light, Sam saw a painted cart pulled onto a grassy strip next to a stream. A pinto horse stood nearby and a young man sat beside it, playing a violin.

He's serenading his horse, Sam thought. *And who could blame him?*

The mare might have stepped out of a fairy tale.

Thick forelock veiled a face that was half dark and half light. The mane draping her to the shoulder could have been a swath of night sky with a beam of starlight white running through its middle.

What a great horse, Sam thought, and gave Ace a guilty pat on the neck, just in case he'd read her mind and felt jealous.

Read all the books about the

Phantom Stallion

Phantom Stallion

◈ 23 ◈

Gypsy Gold

TERRI FARLEY

HarperTrophy®
An Imprint of **HarperCollins**Publishers*

Thanks to Lynn Strauman of Gypsy Rose Ranch for my love-at-first-sight glimpse of Gypsy Vanner horses, and to Dennis Thompson and his late wife, Cindy, who spotted a magical Gypsy Vanner stallion grazing the green fields of Wales and brought him home. To see the real horses behind the fictional one in this book, visit GypsyGold.com and GVHwest.com.

Gypsy Gold

Copyright © 2006 by Terri Sprenger-Farley

Library of Congress Catalog Card Number: 2006920323
ISBN-10: 0-06-081540-X — ISBN-13: 978-0-06-081540-0

❖

First Harper Trophy edition, 2006

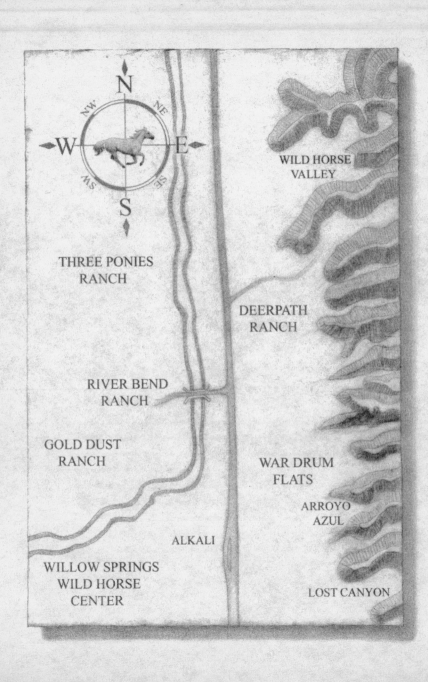

Chapter One ⤫

*I*f there could be such a thing as a second summer, this was it.

Samantha Forster lay on her back in the warm grass and gazed at a cloud Pegasus. Drifts of white made up the mane and tail and gray-edged clumps looked like muscular shoulders. If not for the cloud wings trimmed with sun gold, he'd look like the Phantom.

The mustang stallion could be watching from a nearby ridge or peering through a screen of pinion pines. Sam lay totally still, wishing he'd appear.

Sam's jeans felt hot against her legs. Her head was pillowed on her jacket. Her outspread arms were bare to the green shoots poking up between the brittle autumn grass left uneaten by deer, antelope, or wild horses over the summer.

Why hadn't the cold nighttime temperatures kept the baby grass from pushing up from the warm darkness of the dirt? Why didn't the grass have more sense than to explore where its tender tips would be frozen off any night now?

Sam smiled and closed her eyes. She basked in the sun's warmth and studied the scarlet network of veins crisscrossing the inside of her eyelids. She must be half asleep if she was actually asking herself why grass didn't have the sense to stay underground.

Right now, though, being half asleep was a good thing. She'd promised her best friend, Jen Kenworthy, that she'd play dead for at least an hour.

The two girls had ridden out from River Bend Ranch on Ace and Silly after school the day before.

Armed with a hand-drawn map from Jen's Advanced Biology teacher, the girls had searched for the turkey vultures' roost yesterday on an offshoot of the trail up to Cowkiller Caldera. At dusk, they'd found a tree filled with the black birds.

"Oh, yeah!" Jen had rejoiced and her excitement had electrified her palomino. She'd had to turn the mare in circles to keep her from bolting. Once her mount had settled, Jen had whispered, "We'll be back in the morning."

Grinning without opening her eyes, Sam recalled that Jen hadn't been talking to her. Only her best friend would make a promise to turkey vultures.

They'd turned their horses around, walked back down the hillside, and pitched camp far enough away that they wouldn't disturb the birds.

Jen had researched turkey vultures and come to the conclusion that they were totally misunderstood. She'd vowed to do firsthand research for her project so that she didn't repeat any other scientists' mistakes. That firsthand research included luring the birds near enough that she could sketch them.

Now Jen and Sam were lying still as corpses, hoping a curious turkey vulture would actually land beside them and hop close enough to satisfy its curiosity.

"They have such good senses of smell, they'll know we're not dead," Jen whispered beside her.

Sam rolled her eyes as far to the left as she could without moving her head. She saw blond braids and a tanned face, but Jen's lips didn't seem to move.

"Won't smell rotten enough," Sam joked.

"Sam," Jen said patiently, "they only eat freshly dead things."

"I didn't know buzzards were so picky," Sam teased.

"There are no buzzards in the United States," Jen hissed. "Now we have to hush. Any minute, they could fly off for South America. This flock is rare. It could be the one that stays in Nevada through October."

Sam pressed her lips together, telling herself this flock of turkey vultures wasn't the only thing that was rare. She'd bet there weren't two other teenagers in the country getting their pre-Halloween thrills by offering themselves as bird bait.

Still, Sam was glad Jen had coaxed her into sharing these peaceful moments.

Sam's life had been hamster-on-a-wheel crazy since she'd moved back to northern Nevada from San Francisco. She never would have thought of soaking up October sunshine in a meadow that would soon be blasted by winter storms.

This was a great escape after almost a month of being grounded.

For four long weeks she'd done what she was told—morning chores, school, afternoon chores, and homework—over and over again. She'd learned her lesson this time. She wouldn't do anything to make Dad, Gram, and Brynna worry. Although sometimes it was impossible to tell what would set them off.

Her only fun during those long weeks had come from perfecting her bareback riding skills on her bay mustang Ace.

Since she wasn't allowed to leave the ranch on horseback, she'd sat on him in the corral, trying to find a perfect balance that didn't involve squeezing her legs and accidentally sending him forward.

One afternoon Dallas, River Bend's foreman, had finally asked, "You gonna roost on that horse all night?"

It had sounded like heaven to Sam. What could be cozier than spending the night on Ace, leaning forward with her arms around his neck and her cheek leaning against his mane?

She and Ace had come a long way together since she'd returned from San Francisco. She'd come home a totally timid rider. If she was a cowgirl now, Ace got most of the credit. He'd tricked and bullied her until she knew that if she didn't take charge, he would.

He'd never be a push-button horse, but she loved him with all her heart.

Sam sighed. Jen shushed her again.

Sam raised her eyelashes a tenth of a millimeter and saw three turkey vultures riding the air currents above her.

Cross-shaped black bodies circled, mimicking Sam's own position. Except, in place of arms, they had wide, prehistoric-looking wings. Sam wanted to believe they were just as afraid of her as she was of them, but what if the vultures really mistook her for a dead thing?

It could happen. She remembered a Thanksgiving when she was a little kid, when she'd mistaken a plastic grape for the real thing.

Gram had arranged the pretty red plastic grapes in a Thanksgiving cornucopia. Sam had snatched one and chomped down on it before anyone caught her ruining the centerpiece. With the plastic burning her taste buds, Sam had spit it out. Then her sense of betrayal had turned to anger.

What if the vultures swooped in for brunch, discovered she was faking, then grabbed her with their talons and pecked out her eyes?

"Quit freaking out," Jen hissed.

"I'm not," Sam answered.

"Okay," Jen breathed, but those two syllables managed to say Jen was not convinced.

Sam reminded herself she loved animals. All animals.

Vultures just did what they were born to do. Sure they stuck their heads and necks inside dead bodies, but Jen claimed turkey vultures also spent three hours a day cleaning their feathers—preening, she'd called it.

Sam and Jen had agreed that was a lot longer than either of them ever spent trying to look pretty.

Sam forced air from her lungs and tried to lie flatter. She felt the bumps of the herringbone braid Jen had plaited into her hair this morning, and the tickle of what might be ant feet crossing the nape of her neck, but she lay still.

In the quiet, she heard her shirt move with her breath, then listened as a horse blew through his lips.

Down the hillside, Ace and Silly were getting restless.

Jen had packed into the wilderness with horses more often than Sam, so when Jen insisted on feeding the horses hay instead of grain so they wouldn't be pumped up with energy and dig holes at the camp-site, they'd done it. When Jen pointed out that maps and memories could be faulty and they should water the horses every time there was a chance, they'd done that, too.

Only Jen's decision to tie Ace and Silly to a picket line instead of hobbling them made Sam uneasy. She loved Jen's palomino, Silk Stockings, but there was a reason the mare's nickname was Silly.

Still, the horses had stayed tied all night and all morning while Jen cooked a skillet full of biscuits.

Talk about preening! Sam thought. Jen had brought along premade biscuits just in case hers didn't work out, but it turned out she didn't need them.

Using her mom's cast-iron skillet, Jen had cooked up crisp, golden biscuits that were tender in the middle and delicious.

As Sam thought of the extra biscuits they'd wrapped up and saved for lunch, her stomach growled. Apparently that didn't bother the vultures.

A faint coolness made Sam's eyes spring open. One of the turkey vultures had moved closer. It glided near enough that she saw its head tilt.

That bird knew very well she wasn't dead meat, but it wanted to see what she was.

Pop!

At the sound, all three birds rose higher into the sky.

A horse squealed.

Pop! Pop!

Sitting up, Jen gasped, "Were those shots?"

"I don't know." Sam lurched to her feet, heart pounding.

They weren't shots. Of course they weren't.

She wet her lips and stared at Jen. Behind her glasses, Jen's eyes were wide and worried.

"Should we go see?" Jen asked.

Her uncertainty surprised Sam. Jen was a rancher's daughter and a cowgirl to the bone. Still, Jen was sensible. She wanted sufficient information before she made a move.

They both listened hard.

"If it was a gun, going toward it is the last thing we should—" Sam's voice broke off at the thudding of hooves.

Their horses were loose!

Something clattered, rolled, and shattered. Metal rang from impact and then the sound of hoofbeats faded.

"Let's go!" Jen shouted.

Grabbing her jacket, Sam broke into a run and Jen matched her steps.

Beyond the pounding of their feet, the girls could still hear the hooves.

"They're running away," Jen said in a wondering tone.

Sam took longer strides as she yelled in agreement, "And it's a long walk home!"

The campsite was weirdly quiet.

The horses were gone. Running after them and shouting for them to stop would only make them gallop farther and faster.

Together, Sam and Jen stood, hands on hips, and looked around the clearing.

It was easy to see what had happened. The carefully strung picket line snaked across the campsite, pulled down by the spooked horses before they trampled the sleeping bags.

Sam bent to retrieve her sleeping bag. Hooves had flung it into the dead campfire.

"Do you know how glad I am we doused the fire before leaving?" Sam muttered. She shook out the sleeping bag and brushed at the smear left by charred sticks and ashes, but then she shuddered.

If they'd left the campfire burning after breakfast, the sleeping bag could have been kicked into the embers by the horses, and blazed into flames. Fire could have spread to Jen's sleeping bag, then to their supplies. The whole hillside might have caught fire.

The handle had shattered off Jen's blue pottery mug, but her mom's skillet was where she'd left it, propped against a rock to dry after she'd washed it. Alongside the skillet were their stacked tin plates.

In fact, only three things—the picket line, sleeping bag, and cup—were out of place. The campsite looked pretty orderly except for the white ooze.

"The biscuits," Jen moaned. She pointed at the foil-wrapped tubes, which had split open to let sticky dough escape.

"Refrigerated biscuits," Sam corrected, and they both threw their hands up in disbelief.

Why hadn't one of them thought of this before? Kept cool, the dough waited quietly in those tubes. But the morning sun had heated through the cardboard. The dough inside had risen, expanded, and popped the tubes open.

"At least it wasn't gunshots," Jen said.

Sam nodded. Last month's encounter with a rifle was enough to last a lifetime. She'd faced a horse rustler with a gun and she never wanted to do it again.

The memory made her hands tremble. She inhaled a shaky breath and sat down on a boulder.

"Are you okay?" Jen asked, examining her with an analytical stare.

"I will be," Sam said.

She concentrated on the scent of lingering campfire smoke and the herbal freshness of the pinion trees. Gram and her church friends had harvested pinion pine nuts just last weekend. Gram had been toasting them in the oven when Sam had returned home from school the day before yesterday.

The remembered scent made Sam's pulse settle down.

"Sorry," Sam said, looking up at Jen.

Her friend waved the apology away.

"Go ahead and rest." Jen meant it, but she was striding around camp, picking things up and arranging them in her backpack. "I have to go after Silly. I don't know what she'll do out there."

Jen's palomino mare was a ranch horse. Beautiful, strong, and surprisingly sensible in parades, she was used to sharing pastures and corrals with the other Kenworthy palominos—not running wild.

And no matter how much Jen joked about her horse being neurotic, they loved each other.

As soon as Jen had crawled out of her sleeping bag that morning, the mare had fussed for her touch. When Jen had drawn near enough, Silly had rested her head on Jen's shoulder and left it there, eyes peaceful as Jen stoked her.

Now, Jen knelt to roll up her sleeping bag. She wasn't about to wait for the horses to return. She was breaking camp.

"I think—" Sam broke off, shaking her head.

"Yes?" Jen asked, pausing.

"I wonder which one of them will lead." Sam gestured down the trail. "They both know the way home."

As Jen mulled that over, Sam thought about Ace.

She didn't blame her horse for taking off when she wasn't there to tell him not to, but really, he'd been through police horse desensitization training and tolerated all kinds of weird stuff. Why would he panic at the sound of popping dough?

She thought of the snort she'd heard earlier. Ace had been ready to move on.

If she'd been standing here, holding his reins, turning him to look toward the sound, allowing him to study its source with both eyes, he would have stayed. But she'd been up the hill, so he'd taken the excuse to flee, leaving her afoot.

Sam shook her head. When you hung around with horses, you never got bored. They came up with something new every single day.

"I think they'll stay together, but we've got to go after them," Jen insisted. Then, wistfully, she added, "I'm pretty sure we've seen the last of the turkey vultures, so we might as well."

Sam had forgotten all about the birds, but Jen's shoulders sagged as she gazed into the blue sky. Except for a few long drifts of clouds, it was empty.

"Did you see enough?" Sam asked.

Jen shrugged.

Sam placed a knee on her sleeping bag to hold it closed while she knotted the strings. She tried to think of something that would cheer Jen up.

"At least the horses are saddled," she said.

After breakfast, they'd saddled up to ride to the

roosting tree, but Jen had changed her mind. She'd decided the turkey vultures would be less suspicious of two motionless humans without horses.

"Good point," Jen said, but then she looked around them. "You know all that gear they carried up the mountain?"

Sam tried not to think about it. "We can do it," she said. "And we'll be walking downhill." Sam was trying to sound upbeat, but then she swallowed, feeling a little thirsty.

"Tell me again why we filled our canteens and left them hanging on our saddles?" she moaned.

"We still have that," Jen said, pointing at their big plastic water jug.

Though it was only half full, the jug would be heavy.

"Want to drink it here? It's not like we're going to die of dehydration," Sam said.

Jen pressed an index finger to the bridge of her glasses and cleared her throat as if Sam's words might come back to haunt them.

Sam rushed on, "All we have to do is take the trail back down to the road. If we don't see the horses by then, someone will drive by."

When Jen didn't agree, Sam grabbed the jug and swished it around. Then, as if to seal a promise, she gulped half the water, and handed the jug to Jen.

"Here's to you, partner," Jen joked.

She drank, wiped her wet lips with the back of

her hand, then flattened the empty jug, folded it, and slipped it inside her backpack.

Stomachs sloshing and backs draped with gear, the girls started downhill.

Sam kept her eyes fixed on the trail ahead.

She would not look back. It was melodramatic and stupid to think that the vultures were stalking them.

And if they were, she didn't want to know.

Chapter Two ❧

 am and Jen trudged down the hillside, trading the big iron skillet back and forth.

"This is *my* school project and *I* chose to bring that heavy pan, so let me carry it," Jen protested, when she caught Sam trying to adjust her backpack to the weight of the skillet.

"You didn't see me turning down those delicious biscuits," Sam said. "This is fair."

Jen didn't say anything, and a single sidelong glance told Sam that her best friend was settling into one of her moods. Because Jen was so smart, she was used to being in control of her life. When she wasn't, she turned gloomy.

"Hey," Sam said. "I still don't get why you're

doing this report on turkey vultures."

Jen hefted the straps of her backpack, tossed each braid back over her shoulders, and glared at Sam. She wasn't fooled by her friend's attempt to distract her.

Sam blew air up under her bangs, then resolved not to do that again. Her breath was too hot to make the gesture much of a relief.

"Okay, I agree that they're misunderstood and they're just doing what vultures do, but how can you do a biology report on that? That has more to do with people than—"

Jen cut her off. "That's not what I'm studying. There's evidence that if vultures eat something that died from sickness, their digestive system actually kills the destructive germs. Neutralizes them," Jen emphasized.

"Really?" Sam asked.

Jen nodded and walked a few steps in silence before she continued, "Think of that. What if science could figure out how they do it? We could help humans and animals resist harmful germs."

They kept plodding along. Jen wore that weird, wondering smile for a couple miles and Sam tried not to brood over the realization that they'd gotten an awfully late start for the miles they might have to travel.

It was past noon, later than either of them had thought, and dust roiled up from each footfall. It was impossible to breathe without taking a whiff of the powdery gray stuff.

Sam coughed, then took one hand away from the straps of her backpack and cupped her hand over her nose and mouth.

Wasn't this just great? Sam's mind grumbled. On her first real escape from the ranch in nearly a month, she was in trouble again.

Her pulse kicked up at the thought of Ace trotting over the bridge to River Bend Ranch. Someone would look up at the sound of hooves, expecting to see her returning. Instead, they'd see a riderless horse.

Sam shuddered. Such a sight would make any rancher's heart stop.

Sam trudged along faster, spurred on by the hope that she and Jen could find the horses before they ran home.

"Where did they go?" Sam yelped about an hour later.

"Who?" Jen asked, wiping her forehead with the back of her hand.

"The hoofprints," Sam said, pointing at the dust before them. She whirled and looked back, then wet her lips and shook her head. She couldn't see any tracks. "I was following them, but Ace and Silly must have veered off the trail."

"I didn't notice," Jen said. She sounded embarrassed

as she fanned the totally-un-Jen-like beige shirt she'd worn so that she wouldn't shock the turkey vultures with her usual brightly colored wardrobe. "I hate to admit it, but you know who we could use right now, don't you?"

"No," Sam said, walking faster.

"Sam," Jen said, stopping to roll the stiffness from her shoulders. "You know what my dad said about Jake?"

"I can't hear you," Sam called back, but Jen's rapid downhill footsteps caught up with her.

"'That boy could track a bee through a blizzard,'" Jen drawled, imitating her dad.

Sam shook her head, clearing her ears of the remark. She didn't want to think about Jake right now. She wanted to find her horse, shuck off her boots, and take a nap. "But why would they do it?"

Jen knew Sam was still talking about the horses, and quit teasing her.

"Something spooked them, of course," Jen said. "Much as I love horses, I sometimes wish their primitive little brains didn't scream 'Run!' at the first sign of trouble. I understand that they developed in a world where there weren't any barbed-wire fences, cars—"

"Or canned biscuits," Sam muttered.

"Yeah," Jen said, sounding gloomy again.

As they crab-stepped down a side hill, Sam tried not to tense up. Even when her boot soles slipped on rocks tiny as gravel, she kept her knees from locking. All she needed was to slide down this slope on the seat of her jeans.

Sundown came and the girls were still walking, not riding.

"We should be coming to another road pretty soon," Sam said. "I'm really—"

"Quit apologizing," Jen ordered.

Sam pressed her lips together, but she couldn't stop feeling guilty. She'd insisted they sit for an hour, then two, by the last dirt road they'd crossed.

"It made sense," Jen assured her. "And it was a good place for a lunch break."

"Really, this summer when I drove up that road with Ryan—" Sam started.

"Sam, quit it."

"—we saw Karl Mannix driving on it with the Hummer and then I drove back up there with Sheriff Ballard. That's three trucks traveling on that road in one day. I don't know why, today, we didn't see a single, solitary car, truck, or minivan...." Sam's voice cracked.

Jen gave Sam a quick, one-armed hug before grabbing her by both shoulders and turning her so they faced each other.

"Samantha, honey," Jen said with forced sweetness. "You need to shut up now. No one's expecting us back until tomorrow morning, we know what we're doing, and horses have been taking care of themselves for the last million years or so."

Eyes locked, the girls had a staredown.

Sam lost.

"Your glasses are really dirty," she said.

"I'll scratch the lenses if I polish them with my shirt," Jen replied.

At last, Sam sighed. "I guess you're right. And if the horses don't go home, I'm not in trouble."

She tried to sound like that would be a good thing, but she didn't want Ace and Silly running loose in tack that could endanger them in the wild.

"We can go without water for at least another twenty-four hours, and by then we will have encountered some sort of civilization."

Sure, Sam thought, *if one of us doesn't twist an ankle, or get bitten by a rattlesnake.*

"And we're not lost," Jen said adamantly.

"Did I say we were?"

"Just don't go veering off this path," Jen said.

"Why would I do that?"

"Well, if you saw the Phantom—"

"He's too smart to be out on this hillside where anyone could see him," Sam insisted.

"But look down the hill at all that vegetation," Jen said. Then, she added, "I'm thirsty. I wish we hadn't eaten those biscuit sandwiches."

"Not me," Sam said. Though the biscuits stuffed with cheese had been salty when you had nothing to

drink, they'd tasted great and Sam knew those calo-
ries had helped keep them going all day.

"Did you hear that?" Jen asked. She grabbed
Sam's arm and held her still.

Sam winced at the strength of Jen's grip.

The ground beneath their boots had hardened.
Off to their left was a grove of cottonwood trees.
That meant they were near water, but Sam didn't
hear it flowing. Even when she concentrated with her
eyes closed, she heard nothing but a breeze and
maybe the far-off howling of coyotes.

"This way," Jen said. She shrugged her backpack
into a more comfortable position and stepped off the
path.

"Wait! You were the one—"

Jen peered through the darkness, then strode off
through the short, crunchy grass.

"Uh-uh," Sam said. "No. We can't leave the trail."

"Just for a few yards," Jen called back.

"I bet that's what the Donner party said," Sam
muttered.

"What?" Jen asked, but her steps didn't slow and
the blond braids bouncing against her back finally
faded from view.

Should she follow Jen? Half her brain said there
was no sense in both of them getting lost. The other
half reasoned that since it was full dark now and they
had their sleeping bags, it would be a good idea to

make camp off the trail and keep searching for the horses at dawn.

Besides, Sam thought as she hurried in the direction she was pretty sure Jen had taken, she was a loyal friend.

Brush cracked underfoot and she was looking down, trying to be careful where she set her boots, when Jen's outline loomed up in front of her.

Automatically, her hands came up to keep from running into her friend.

"Sam!" Jen whispered urgently. "Listen."

Finally Sam heard it. The melody could have been made by waving branches and soprano winds, but the sounds recurred in patterns. A bit lower than the other sounds, a human voice was singing.

Chills drizzled down Sam's neck.

I'm not going over there.

She'd already opened her mouth to warn Jen that this was too weird, when she heard a stamp and a familiar snort.

"That's Ace," Sam whispered.

Suddenly her feet didn't hurt and she'd changed her mind about going on. She slipped past Jen and rushed through the blackness as if magnetized to her horse.

Jen followed so closely, Sam hoped she wouldn't stomp on her heel and make them both fall. But neither of them stumbled and the grove around them began showing more clearly. Sam saw bark and leaves as they crept up on their horses.

After a few more steps their mounts' silhouettes took form. She could tell that the horses were still saddled.

Silly's flaxen mane and Quarter Horse conformation showed first, but Ace was there, too. Silly blocked most of the firelight, but a bit of brightness touched Ace's bay coat and the white star on his forehead.

Sam sucked in her stomach and held her breath as she stepped over a rock.

Jen moved so quietly, Sam couldn't even hear her. With only a few more yards left between them and the horses, there was no reason for their silence. The horses didn't seem to care that they were coming.

Ace and Silly must be tired, hungry, and ready to be caught, or they would have bolted. They had to have sensed the girls' approach, but both horses kept their heads high, ears pricked toward the singing cowboy or camper or whatever he was.

And it was a he. Sam could hear that much.

Just a few more steps. Then she could grab Ace and go.

But gooseflesh prickled all over her body as Sam realized something eerie was going on.

Ace was a mustang. Once he escaped, he was not this easy to recapture. Why was he just standing here?

Sam clamped her hand on the right rein, near the bit. She had him!

Ace lifted his chin a mere inch and flicked one ear her way.

Sam rubbed the bay's neck. It was cool beneath the sweat-stiff hair. Maybe he was just worn out.

Sam tried to back her horse, but he resisted.

She clucked her tongue for him to come along. He didn't.

Then she glanced in the direction her horse was staring and caught her breath.

No, Sam decided, her horse wasn't exhausted. He was spellbound.

Chapter Three ❧

Smoke twisted up from a campfire. By its light, Sam saw a painted cart pulled onto a grassy strip next to a stream. A pinto horse stood nearby and a young man sat beside it, playing a violin.

He's serenading his horse, Sam thought. *And who could blame him?*

The mare might have stepped out of a fairy tale.

Thick forelock veiled a face that was half dark and half light. The mane draping her to the shoulder could have been a swath of night sky with a beam of starlight white running through its middle.

Tall and thickly muscled, the mare still looked cute, not intimidating—maybe because of the fuzzy black tufts showing inside her ears or the white hair curling soft and fine above those massive hooves.

One of her hooves wouldn't fit inside my hat, Sam thought. *It would flatten it.*

The mare's sloping shoulders promised a smooth ride, and Sam pictured the horse carrying a runaway princess. In fact, the big black-and-white paint could carry a princess *and* a prince on her broad and gleaming back.

What a great horse, Sam thought, and gave Ace a guilty pat on the neck, just in case he read her mind and felt jealous.

The mare watched the musician's bow stroke haunting music from his violin. Then, as the tempo built in liveliness, the paint nodded instead of clapping along.

The words of the song weren't easy to make out. Some might have been in another language, but after two repetitions, Sam could have sung along with the refrain.

"Gypsy gold does not clink and glitter, oh no. It gleams in the sun and neighs in the dark, ah yes."

He really was singing to his horse, and the feeling he put into the words made Sam shiver. She cast a quick glance at Jen, but the firelight reflected on the lenses of her glasses made it hard to tell what she was thinking.

Was she as taken in by the music? Ace and Silly were, that was for sure, but Sam spotted one creature that wasn't captivated.

The colt was no more than six months old. His compact body and sturdy legs looked tawny dun.

When a breeze plucked sparks from the campfire and spun them over the colt's head, he snapped at them. When they drifted out of reach, he sneezed and switched his short tail in boredom, but an instant later he was darting around the paint mare, past the musician and out of the ring of light.

What had gotten into him? The colt was about Tempest's age and Sam knew that sometimes a jolt of high spirits just made young horses run for the joy of it.

Not this time, though.

Sam's eyes followed the colt as he crashed toward shifting shadows on the other side of the campfire.

Animals, Sam thought. Lots of them.

She caught the flow of manes and the flash of startled eyes.

Mustangs?

Fingers of firelight stretched far enough that Sam was pretty sure she made out coats of blood bay, black, and roan.

She could hardly believe her eyes. The Phantom's band was clustered in the cottonwood grove.

It wasn't that the herd was out of its territory. The horses had ranged between the La Charla River and Cowkiller Caldera before. But they were so close. The whole herd clustered no more than two dozen yards away from this stranger.

Sam's mind grappled with surprise while her eyes kept searching. She sorted through the forms of mares and half-grown colts until she found him.

The stallion stood apart from the others. If a drop of moon dew had fallen through the branches to land glowing in the grove, it wouldn't have been brighter than the Phantom. He shone silver in the dark woods.

Sam's breath caught, and without meaning to, her hand rose to press against her chest. Could extra blood surge through your heart at the sight of the horse you loved? To her, it felt like it could, but she didn't call to him. All she wanted was to watch him.

Tense, with every nerve alert, the silver stallion was poised to run, but he'd turned one ear toward the music.

Did the melody stir memories of the years he'd lived as a captive horse? Was that why he wasn't afraid of the stranger?

It wasn't the pinto mare that had lured the stallion. If it had been, he would have been staring and snorting. Instead, he listened.

Protector of his band, wild with his tangled mane and predator's eyes, every inch an untamed beast, the Phantom still couldn't resist the soaring notes.

Sam remembered Dallas, their ranch foreman, saying that when she'd been away in San Francisco, he'd sat on the bunkhouse steps at night, playing his harmonica. Sometimes, if he squinted just right, he'd seen a lonely horse listening as the music floated across to the wild side of the river.

Sam knew the horse had been the Phantom. The stallion was so drawn by music, she'd once called him to her by singing an off-key and trembling Christmas carol.

The musician at the fireside gave no sign that he'd noticed his audience. He played on while the adventurous colt sidled among the mustangs. Then the enchantment ended.

Irritated squeals and snapping teeth drove the colt away. Hooves tramped, horsehide struck bark, and the little dun gave a high-pitched whinny.

"Poor baby," Sam whispered.

Clumsy in his sad retreat, the colt bolted beyond the mustangs' reach and veered toward the campfire.

Watch out! Sam's eyes had widened, but she hadn't managed to yell a warning when the violin bow slid screeching across the strings and the musician's out-flung arm blocked the colt.

Spooked, the colt wheeled away from the campfire and bucked, flinging his heels at the night sky. The mustangs trotted away, disturbed but not terrified. The pinto mare seemed quietly amused.

Without halter or hobbles, she stepped back from the colt's commotion and swung her heavy head to face Jen and Sam.

The mare's eyelashes were black on one side and white on the other. She looked like she was winking at them.

The musician retrieved his fallen instrument from the dirt, then stood, holding his violin and bow against his side, as he greeted them.

"Welcome to my camp."

When he spoke, he looked younger.

Maybe eighteen or nineteen, Sam thought as she and Jen led their horses into the clearing.

"Hi," she and Jen said together.

The guy watched with a calm smile that seemed more like his usual expression rather than anything to do with them.

He was medium height and had black hair that was mostly smooth with random curls behind his ears, brown-gold skin, and dark eyes with the longest lashes Sam had ever seen.

How much would he have been teased about that in school? Sam wondered.

Stop smiling, Sam told herself. Remember the warnings pounded into your brain cells during Stranger Danger classes in elementary school.

Or take a lesson from Jen. She was acting polite but cautious.

But all Sam had to do was swing into Ace's saddle and she'd be out of here. Sure, they were out in the middle of Nevada late at night, but the guy's attention had already wandered back to his violin, checking it for scratches.

He cradled it like a baby before looking up at them to say, "I wondered when you would get here."

"You knew we were coming?" Sam asked.

"Of course," he said, inclining his head toward Ace and Silly.

"Two saddled and bridled horses?" Jen said, and now she did smile. "I guess it makes sense that someone would be coming after them."

"Oh yeah," Sam said, laughing at herself.

Then they just stood there: two girls with two horses, one guy with two horses.

Moving quickly to slip his violin inside his cart, the young man gestured for them to make themselves at home.

"My name is Nicolas Raykov," he said, shaking each girl's hand. "I'm driving from Seattle to Sacramento with my partner Lace."

Nicolas had no accent, but Sam heard a formal cadence in his words. She didn't take time to analyze it.

"That must be seven hundred miles," Jen said, before she introduced herself.

"Eight hundred, if you don't count detours," Nicolas said.

"The weather's going to be changing soon," Sam warned.

Lots of people thought Nevada's high desert was hot all the time. In fact, it was so changeable, she'd learned not to assume the seasons meant anything.

"It already is," Nicolas said. "But I've planned for it. We'll be in Sacramento before the snows fly." He gave his mare's neck a hearty pat. "I've promised Lace."

Then, just after Sam and Jen had introduced themselves and their horses, Ace raked his teeth across the feed pack tied on behind Silly's saddle.

With an offended squeal, Silly raised a hind leg, swished her tail, and bared her teeth at the bay gelding.

"Ace!" Sam tugged at the reins, pulling her horse's head away.

Amazed at Silly's short-tempered response, Jen apologized to Nicolas. "They're hungry. We'd better feed them before they get into a real squabble."

"Please, help yourself to some hay. Lace is quite generous," Nicolas said, "and I have plenty of food to share with you, as well."

"They carried their own food," Jen explained as she unpacked. "And we have dinner with us."

It wasn't much of a dinner, but Sam didn't say so.

Jen had insisted on bringing a canned meal of beans with hot dogs cut up in them and she wanted to eat them cold, right out of the can, accompanied only by soda crackers. The idea grossed Sam out, but Jen had said it was what she'd eaten with her dad when they'd gone on pack trips into the mountains. She'd insisted it was a meal fit for real cowgirls. Sam couldn't make herself agree, but before they'd left, she'd had a stern talk with herself. Since it was only one dinner out of her entire life, she could go along with her best friend.

Jen was uncharacteristically clumsy with the can

opener, probably because she was watching Nicolas while she fumbled with it. Sam couldn't stop glancing at him, either. Something about Nicolas and Lace made Sam imagine they'd come into this clearing out of another time.

Finally, Jen got the can open, and Sam was hungry enough that the beans tasted fine. Afterward, Nicolas boiled water and served them hot mint tea. Sipping it as she sat on a rock near the campfire, Sam felt almost at home.

Jen swept a few twigs and leaves aside to clear a seat on the ground and leaned her back against a boulder. Nicolas sat across from them, on the other side of the fire. Lace wandered loose around the camp, touching noses with Ace and Silly.

"She is so friendly," Sam marveled.

"Good old Lace," Nicolas said proudly. At once, the mare's head swung to look at him. "You like the company, don't you, girl?" To Sam and Jen, he added, "It's been just the two of us for over a month."

"Don't you mean three?" Jen asked. She pointed to the colt peering from under Lace's neck.

"Him? That little one's not an official member of our caravan. He fell in with us about two weeks ago, between—" Nicolas paused. He seemed to be mentally retracing their journey. "Good Thunder Meadows and Susanville."

Good Thunder Meadows had a familiar ring to it, but Sam couldn't decide why.

"He's awfully young to be on his own," Jen said.

"We searched for his mother," Nicolas said. "There'd been a lightning storm and I feared . . ."

Nicolas glanced toward the colt, then shrugged. Sam and Jen understood his hint that the foal's mother might have been killed by lightning.

"Hmm," Jen said, and Sam guessed her scowl was for whoever had failed to keep track of the vulnerable young animal.

"I talked with a sheepherder, two days north of here, who called him a 'bummer' foal. He suggested the colt was orphaned and had fallen in with some mustangs and just sneaked meals from whichever mares would have him."

Sam had heard of bummer calves and lambs, but never a bummer colt.

"From what we just saw," Jen said, gesturing to the spot where the Phantom's herd had been, "that seems unlikely."

"I don't know," Sam said, trying to take the sting out of Jen's remark. "Those wild mares wouldn't make it easy for an outsider because he's old enough to be weaned. But when he was younger, they might have fed him. Remember Mistress Mayhem?"

Jen had picked up a twig and she took her time examining the autumn leaves that still clung to it before she nodded.

"A friend of ours has a colt that was temporarily adopted by a burro," Sam explained to Nicolas, but there was something else about the dun colt, all alone on the range, that started a niggling thought in her brain.

"Lace is tolerant when he noses around her flank, but he was very disappointed to find she couldn't be his nursemaid. Still, he seems to have found enough food to get by."

Sam wanted a good look at the colt, but he stayed flat against the paint's black-and-white barrel. No matter where she wandered, he pressed to the side farthest from the people.

Jen tossed the twig she'd been twirling toward the fire.

"What do you call him?" Jen asked.

"He's not mine to name." Nicolas sounded surprised. "I hope he'll go back to the wild ones, because soon we'll be trotting along the roadside, with traffic buzzing by."

Recalling the colt's heedless rush across the clearing, Sam hoped so, too.

"You're right. We're not far from the highway," Sam said.

"Or home," Jen added pointedly.

"Yeah," Sam said, but she wasn't sure she had enough energy to ride the rest of the way tonight.

While Jen explained the purpose of their trip and the unplanned "adventure" of the last eight hours, she picked up another stick and poked the leafy twig the rest of the way into the campfire.

The leaves burned with a hiss while Sam thought of cuddling down in her own bed.

Nicolas seemed as interested in turkey vultures as Jen, until a coyote's howl nearby made him turn away.

Jen shot Sam a questioning look, but then Nicolas turned back.

"Were you planning to make the rest of your ride tonight?" he asked.

"Yes," Jen answered.

"No," Sam said at the same time.

Nicolas chuckled.

"You're welcome to roll out your sleeping bags at my fireside," he invited.

Sam scooted forward on the boulder and tilted her head to see Jen's face.

"Do you really want to keep going?" Sam asked.

"We've probably seen the last of the turkey vultures," Jen pointed out.

"But Jen, the horses are tired and no one's expecting us until tomorrow."

Jen shot Sam a glare.

Sam sighed. "Okay, I don't want to get in trouble again."

Sam wished she hadn't said that, either. She sounded like a little kid. Still, it was the truth. She couldn't stand being grounded.

But why had Jen suddenly changed the plan?

Was it because their families thought they were

camping up the hill, instead of down in this grove with a stranger? But they'd just seen him ignore the crash of his prized violin to save an orphan foal from being burned. Didn't that mean he was a good guy?

Nicolas shifted his position across the fire. He'd been leaning back on two hands, staring into the flames as the girls talked.

Now he leaned forward. The angle of firelight changed, making a mask of shadows from his brows down to his cheekbones.

"Tell me honestly, Samantha and Jennifer," he said. "Do you feel you must move on because I'm a gypsy?"

Chapter Four ⁊

"You're a gypsy?" Both girls spoke at once.

Sam looked down. She picked at a thread fraying from the stitchings on her jeans. Why had her voice squeaked like she was thrilled? And Jen had sounded startled.

No wonder Nicolas looked confused.

"What did you think?" he asked.

"Nothing," Sam said, but why hadn't her brain picked up the clue from the song? The words had said horses were a gypsy's gold.

Still, she'd sung lots of songs that had nothing to do with her life. Take "Puff, the Magic Dragon," for instance. But Nicolas looked truly interested and a little concerned over why they hadn't known he was a gypsy.

"I probably would have guessed you were Italian," Jen said. "Or Basque. There are lots of Basque families around here."

Sam stared at Nicolas, but she didn't notice anything exotic. In fact, the only thing exceptional about him was that on his otherwise smooth face, there was a wrinkle above his left eyebrow, as if he constantly raised it. What did that mean? That he was skeptical like Jen?

"My ancestors were Greek," Nicolas said, "and my family's been in England for generations. Even though we picked up a Bulgarian last name, we're still gypsies."

"I've never met a gypsy," Sam said, and when Nicolas spread his arms as if he were on display, she blurted, "But you're not from Egypt?"

"Sam!" Jen gave an appalled gasp.

"What?" Sam said, turning toward Jen. "I read somewhere that—well, it kind of makes sense, doesn't it? I mean the words are alike—Egypt and gypsy." When Jen shook her head, Sam looked back at Nicolas. "That's not right?"

"No, and I'm afraid I can't read your palm, either," Nicolas said, snapping his fingers in pretend disappointment. "And if you left any tea leaves in your cup . . . ? I can't tell your future."

Sam's face went hot with embarrassment. Was he mad because she was ignorant?

"Maybe you heard gypsies were pickpockets and con men, too."

Nicolas's grin reminded Sam of some of the cowboys' when she'd first moved back to River Bend Ranch. But she'd kind of understood those superior smiles. They'd known she'd lived in San Francisco, and they'd assumed the boss's citified daughter didn't know anything about ranch life and wouldn't want to learn.

Well, they'd been wrong, and whatever Nicolas was thinking was wrong, too.

"I don't even know what a con man is," Sam said. Her face stung from the deepening blush, but she wasn't about to shut up. "I just thought it was kind of cool, because I've heard gypsies are wizards with horses. That's all."

She couldn't go on with her voice shaking, so she stopped.

"Wizards?" Nicolas asked.

Embarrassment was a black hole. A bottomless black hole, and just when she thought she'd crashed into its floor, another level opened up and down she fell.

Sam looked away from Nicolas and stared into the fire. The leafy twig Jen had fed the flames had charred into a bare stem.

Sam turned toward the grove where the Phantom had stood just minutes ago.

She'd give anything to have galloped away on the stallion's silver back. He'd carry her to a haven where they'd be surrounded by black peaks and countless stars. But no. She was still here, facing a guy who smiled while he made fun of her.

"Look," she said.

"Sam, don't bother. You made a little mistake. Big deal. He's the one who should apologize." Jen flashed Nicolas a hostile look, and though Sam appreciated her friend standing up for her, Jen was making things worse.

For a moment there was silence broken only by the whuffling of horses' lips over the grass.

"You think I owe you an apology?" Nicolas asked.

"Yes!" Sam and Jen said together.

Nicolas shrugged. "I was only teasing."

"You're not very good at it," Jen said, and her sarcasm made all three of them laugh.

"I'm sorry," Nicolas said, still chuckling. Before he went on, Lace plodded up and nosed his shoulder so hard, he nearly tipped over. "You could have given me that hint a bit earlier," Nicolas told the horse. Then he looked from Jen to Sam. "If we can start over, I'll explain."

"Why not," Sam said.

"Sure." Jen didn't sound convinced, but Nicolas went on.

"Mostly, I'm making this journey to discover what

it means to be a gypsy. I'm just a middle-class college kid from Seattle, but my grandparents, who are traditional, old-school gypsies, say that the open road will reveal my heritage to me."

Nicolas said the last few words in a dramatic, almost mocking way.

But, Sam thought, *here he is*.

"My grandparents also said that *ganjo*—non-gypsies, like you," he said apologetically, "would blame me for stuff like stealing chickens or laundry off clotheslines—"

Jen gave a snort of disbelief, then said, "Sorry, but that's ridiculous."

Nicolas shrugged.

"Some places, gypsies have bad reputations based on old folktales. Grandfather remembers traveling in a vardo as a little kid and hiding when people came out of their towns to throw rocks and set dogs on the caravan.

"Grandmother told me a man stole his neighbor's horse and sold it, then blamed the gypsies. Her brother spent a week in jail until they found a witness to what had really happened.

"They convinced me that some people have these stereotypes. . . ." Nicolas's voice trailed off. "So, uh, yeah." He cleared his throat. "I guess I kind of misjudged you before you could do it to me. Sorry."

Sam thought it was one of the best apologies she'd ever heard.

"We hang around with cowboys, so we can take a little joshing," Sam said, even though that wasn't exactly what Nicolas had done.

"I'm glad," he said. "I hardly knew I was a gypsy until my grandparents came to live with us a few years ago. I mean, my father runs a car-repair shop and my mom's the bookkeeper. Neither of them have accents, unless American TV English counts. And even though gypsies are known as Travelers some places, my parents only left England for the U.S. and since then, they've stayed put.

"About the only gypsy tradition they follow," Nicolas added, "is when someone in the family gets sick, they descend on him."

"Descend?" Jen asked.

"Oh, yeah. They crowd the hospital room with aunts, stepbrothers, second cousins . . ."

"That's interesting," Jen said.

"It's weird," Nicolas corrected her. "When one of my uncles was in a motorcycle accident, the doctor had to elbow her way through the crowd and shout to be heard. But my dad told me we were all there to make sure he got the best of care."

A cricket chirred through the darkness. Otherwise, the clearing was still. It was getting late, but Sam had the feeling that she and Jen had both decided to camp out there.

Nicolas's kindness to the horses, his devotion to his quirky family, and his sincere apology to them had gone a long way toward making Sam feel he was trustworthy.

"What do your parents think of you making this trip?" Jen asked.

"They hate it," Nicolas said. "They say the reason gypsies traveled was because they didn't have a place of their own. They say it's not about a love of the open road; it's about prejudice.

"Even though they've told me stories about prejudice, about people siccing their dogs on them, just because they're gypsies and stuff like that, my grandparents gave me Lace for high school graduation and made me a deal."

"What was the deal?" Sam asked.

"If I finished my first semester of college with a B average—" Nicolas broke off. As if he'd noticed a change in Jen's expression, he pointed at her. "Go ahead. Ask."

Sam gave a surprised laugh, but Jen just nodded and asked, "Okay. How were your grades during your first semester of college?"

"I earned a B plus average," Nicolas announced. "It would've been higher, but I thought it would be fun to take a drama class and it turned out everyone in there had been on stage in a zillion high school productions, except for me."

"Okay," Jen said, as if she'd allow such a miscalculation.

"So, they bought me a *vardo*—a caravan wagon,"

he explained, gesturing at the vehicle behind them, "and I spent all my free time from January until June planning my route, learning how to drive, and training Lace."

Once more, he included the horse in the conversation. "But that was the easy part, wasn't it, girl?" Then he looked at Sam and Jen. "Traveling cross-country must be imprinted in their DNA."

"What kind of horse is she?" Sam asked.

"A Gypsy Vanner," Nicolas said proudly. "Officially it's a fairly new breed, but her ancestors have been pulling vardos for generations. First just walking at roadsides, tolerating other horses, riders, and carriages. Then, with the coming of trains, they learned to cross the tracks moments after those loud monsters went by, and finally, they accepted all the racket of cars and trucks."

"She has draft blood, doesn't she?" Jen observed.

Nicolas nodded. "Gypsy Vanners are a combination of black Shire horses and white Dales ponies, according to my grandmother. My grandfather claims that they owe more to trotters with no names except 'champion who wins every time I bet on him.'"

Sam smiled and looked at Ace.

"So they're a lot like mustangs," she said. "A lot of great breeds came together to make one amazing horse."

Nicolas turned toward Ace. "He was once wild?"

"Yep," Sam said proudly.

"But not the palomino," he added.

"No way," Jen said.

Sam took offense, as she always did when Jen acted as if Quarter Horses were better than mustangs, but then Sam thought of the Phantom. He was a mustang more beautiful than any other horse in the world.

"I'm sorry we scared them away—the wild horses," Sam said.

"Don't be," he said. "I was surprised to have them visit again."

Sam didn't tell Nicolas that the Phantom had probably been drawn by his music. Nicolas seemed like a good guy, but she refused to tell anyone anything that would make the stallion more vulnerable.

"I admit that's why I camped here a second night, to see if they'd come back," he said. "Lace is the only horse I really know, and though she pretends to like my music, I'm always wondering if she's just being polite because I'm the keeper of the hay."

So much for my secret, Sam thought. Nicolas had guessed the horses were drawn to his music.

"You do play the violin well," Jen admitted, "and I like the lyrics of your song."

"I can't take credit for that. The tune's a lullaby my grandmother sings, and the saying is from my grandfather. I kind of put them together. I haven't written anything down, so it keeps changing."

"But the horses like it," Jen said.

"They came for the water," Nicolas said, gesturing toward the stream, "and stayed for the entertainment—the best for miles around," he joked.

Just then, all four horses threw their heads high. The colt hid behind Lace.

"Did you hear anything?" Sam asked the others.

"No, but it could be a smell."

Even as Jen spoke, Sam saw Ace's nostrils flare wide and he took a noisy breath.

"It's the coyotes," Nicolas said. "Last night I watched them dancing."

"Dancing?" Jen repeated.

"Maybe I was in the mood to see magic after the wild horses came to my camp last night," Nicolas conceded, "but I saw a female and her pup playing in the moonlight and it looked like they were dancing."

Sam grinned. "Give him a break. He's from Seattle."

"Yeah," Nicolas echoed. "I can take you to where I watched from last night, if you want to take a chance on seeing them again."

"I want to see!" Sam said.

"You can ride double on Lace," Nicolas offered.

"If you're sure she's not too tired from pulling the wagon," Sam said, trying to overcome her bounce of excitement.

"She's been lazing around camp all day. Besides, I've seen her work all day, and then, if she gets excited, jump right off the ground."

"I'm sold," Jen said, then pointed to Sam. "You can drive."

While Sam and Jen tethered Ace and Silly, Nicolas slipped a worn leather bridle onto Lace.

Sam lifted the reins. The connection to the snaffle was instant, but she felt Lace's attention shift to Nicolas as soon as he began walking away from camp.

"She knows where you're going," Sam said.

When Nicolas only nodded, Sam heard the echo of her voice and decided she'd better be quiet. Sneaking up on coyotes would definitely require silence.

Chapter Five ❧

The yapping of coyotes led them to a ridge that overlooked clumps of sagebrush surrounding small, flat places Sam thought of as deer beds.

No deer slept here tonight.

Just as Nicolas had said, coyotes were dancing by starlight.

Gray-brown fur rippled as the coyotes took turns chasing each other. A mother streaked after a half-grown pup. He hurdled over a rock with something in his mouth. The mother cut around the rock at such a speedy slant, her claws scrabbled to hold her upright. The pup circled back. Tongue flying from the corner of her mouth, his mother sprinted after him, moving so fast, she hardly touched the ground.

Coyote tag, Sam thought. Even if they weren't exactly dancing, they played, with no idea humans were watching.

Panting, the pup dropped what he'd held clamped in his teeth and his mother snapped it up. She ran, dropped it to taunt the pup, then dragged it out of his reach. Snapping, he lunged after her, and Sam got a better look at the prize he couldn't wait to recapture.

The thing they tugged and traded was some sort of long-dead, half-eaten creature.

Yuck, Sam thought. This gave new meaning to the idea of playing with your food.

Abruptly, their game turned serious. The female stood with forelegs straddling the mangled treasure. Ears back, she bared her teeth. The fur on her muzzle wrinkled and showed white fangs.

As the pup approached with his head held lower than his shoulders, Sam noticed the light fluffy fur showing like a ruff on his chest.

Tail wagging near to the ground, the pup pretended to be submissive. Mouth open, head turned to one side, he crept toward his mother on bent legs.

Don't hurt me, he seemed to say, but the instant his mother stopped snarling and her upright tail relaxed, he grabbed the scrap. Rejoicing, the pup tossed it into the air.

Sam's fingers itched for a camera. How cool would it be to keep these images forever? She was staring harder, trying to engrave the scene on her brain cells, when barking exploded like applause from the brush down below.

That sounded doggish, Sam thought. In fact, the barks could have been from her dog, Blaze. While she tried to make sense of the sounds, Blaze himself suddenly bounded into the clearing.

She braced herself for a fight, but that hadn't been Blaze's intruder bark. He woofed a greeting at the coyote and her pup.

Sam didn't say a word, but suddenly it all made sense.

She knew where the Border collie had gone all those nights he'd slipped away.

She knew what he'd been longing for as he howled in the moonlight.

The adult coyote was Blaze's mate—and that must be his puppy.

Blaze trotted to the spot where the pup stood guard over the lump of fur. The pup growled, but Blaze ignored his sassiness and chattered little love bites on his back.

It was a display of dominance, but in the sweetest possible way.

It took Jen a few seconds longer to recognize the Border collie, but when she did her intake of breath sounded like ripping cloth.

Suddenly still, the canines tested the air. Then,

though no sign of agreement passed among them, they fled in a rippling run through the night and out of sight.

"That was your dog playing with the coyotes," Jen said, marveling at what she'd seen.

"No," Nicolas said. "You're just trying to trick the city kid. He had to be wild."

"That was Blaze," Sam agreed.

"Wow," Jen went on, "so the pup must be a coydog."

Coydog. Sam turned the word over in her mind, pretty sure she'd never heard it before. It was obvious what it meant, but was a coydog a wild predator or did it come when it was called and lick your face "hello"?

"I don't know anything about coydogs. Do you?" Sam asked, and she noticed that Nicolas's face lost its skeptical look as she consulted Jen.

Jen was thinking. Hands folded together with only the index fingers sticking up, tapping against her lips. Because she planned to be a vet, Jen studied animal behavior and she remembered everything she read.

"Not much." Jen shook her head. "Dad told me they didn't really exist—but obviously he was wrong."

Sam thought about the pup's markings, the coyotes' excitement as Blaze popped out of the brush, and the way he'd joined them.

"Maybe," Sam began, but no more words came to her. There was just no other way to put those puzzle pieces together. The three were a family.

"It's no coincidence," Jen assured Sam. "I've tried thinking about it from different angles, and though Dad told me coyotes would lure dogs away from home by pretending to play with them while the rest of the pack circled up to attack —"

"That was no trap," Sam finished for her.

Lace pawed the dirt in impatience. Sam reached down to pat the pinto's shoulder. Jen reached back and gave the mare a good scratch at the base of her tail.

"I don't mean to brag, but did you notice how she reacted to all that excitement?" Nicolas asked.

"She's great," Sam answered, but she didn't say much more as they returned to the campsite. She couldn't stop thinking of Blaze and the coyotes until an unfamiliar word pulled her back into the conversation.

". . . figured out why I feel an affinity with them," Nicolas was telling Jen.

"Why?" Jen asked. "Don't tell me you eat road-kill and howl at the moon."

"Jen! Now who's being rude?" Sam looked over her shoulder and into Jen's grinning face.

"Rarely," Nicolas teased back, "but there's a European youth group for gypsies called the Coyotes."

"Cool. What do they do?" Jen asked.

While Sam waited for Jen to make another joke, Nicolas strode on ahead, still talking. "Who knows?" he said. "I'd never heard of them until my mom told me not to get mixed up with them. Seeing those coyotes, though . . ." Nicolas's voice trailed off and Sam didn't know him well enough to even guess what he was wishing. "Good thing I'm keeping a journal," he said with a sigh. "I need to write some stuff down."

Back in camp, Sam and Jen unrolled their sleeping bags near the fire.

"Good night, Ace," Sam called to her horse.

"'Night, Silly," Jen told her palomino.

"Let me know if you need anything." Nicolas's voice came muffled from inside the caravan wagon.

He's doing his best to give us privacy, Sam thought.

She tried not to imagine what Dad would say if he could see her now. Without a doubt, he'd disapprove.

Not because Nicolas was a gypsy, Sam thought, but because he was a stranger.

Gram and Brynna would probably agree with Dad, though she couldn't picture either of them caring that Nicolas was a gypsy either.

"After all our walking," Jen muttered as she wiggled down in her sleeping bag, "you'd think I'd be sore, but I'm just sleepy."

"Yeah," Sam said, but she wasn't sleepy. Her thoughts bounced like a ping-pong ball as she wondered how people would react to a gypsy wagon rumbling through Darton County.

Sam couldn't guess what Dallas, Pepper, and Ross would think about Nicolas. The cowboys would see him as an outsider, but he was good to his horse. Predicting Linc Slocum's reaction was easy. He criticized other people, hoping no one noticed he was the real problem. Jake would be cool with Nicolas and so would Sam's family. Gram's friend Mrs. Allen liked teenagers. Besides, she was preoccupied right now with her fiancé and their plans for a new program at Blind Faith Mustang Sanctuary.

Nicolas's grandparents had warned him about racism, and though Sam wished people had progressed past that, she knew they hadn't.

Sam twisted onto her other side, turning her face away from the fire's heat.

For most of her childhood, she'd thought all racists were nasty, bad-smelling people, because of one ugly moment. Not long after Mom had died, Jake's family had taken Sam to the fair. Looking back, Sam knew they were trying to distract her from Dad's grief and her own confusion, but she'd been having fun. She didn't even remember Jake protesting when his parents ordered him to hold hands with her so she wouldn't get lost.

The trouble had begun when a man tried to cut between them.

First, Sam had noticed his unwashed smell. Next,

his paper plate of greasy food had dropped from his hands. She and Jake had jumped back, looked up at a man's angry face.

"I hanker for fried liver all year long, and because of you"—he'd snarled at Jake—"you little red—"

Sam told herself she didn't remember what he'd said next, but the man's head had jutted toward Jake. His eyes had squinted, and his open, sneering mouth made her fear he was about to spit. At them.

"Sam!"

Startled, she rolled over to see that Jen had risen up on one elbow. "Are you having a nightmare?"

It took a few seconds, but finally Sam said, "Yeah, sort of."

"You're okay," Jen said drowsily.

Sam sighed, and as she fell asleep she couldn't help wishing all bad people wore a stink. That way, it would be easier to identify them and keep them out of your life.

Chapter Six ❧

The first thing Sam saw when she opened her eyes the next morning was the black-and-white face of Lace.

Breathing sweet hay breath and plucking at Sam's hair with her nimble lips, the mare inspected her.

"Hello, pretty girl," Sam mumbled, and when she raised her hand to touch the mare's gleaming black cheek, Lace didn't pull away.

The colt beside her did, though, and the skitter of his hooves woke Sam the rest of the way.

Yawning, she crawled out of her sleeping bag and noticed Jen, standing at the back of the gypsy wagon, watching herself in a suspended mirror as she braided her hair.

Jen must have caught Nicolas's reflection as he approached, because she didn't look away from the mirror as she said, "Ah, he cooks."

"No, but I boil water," Nicolas said as he handed Jen a brown mug, "and my mom believes a strong cup of English tea can put any trouble right."

Sam listened to their voices as she sat on her sleeping bag, but she turned her attention to her feet.

This was the kind of frosty fall morning Gram liked. She said it had "snap."

In Sam's opinion, it had *teeth*. Cold gnawed through her shirt and jeans. It nibbled on her fingers, making her so shivery and uncoordinated, she couldn't hold her boot still to aim her socked foot into it.

Nicolas's knuckles were red as if he'd scrubbed them, but Sam was more interested in the steam curling up from the mug he offered her. Spiced with the aroma of oranges, the tea beckoned her to drink. Sam almost tipped the mug in her eagerness to grab it.

She sipped and swallowed. The hot drink thawed her windpipe, fingers, and brain.

Feeling more awake, Sam set the cup aside to pull on her second boot. She pushed her hair back from her eyes, tucked it neatly behind her ears, and looked at Nicolas.

He held a box of cold cereal and bowls, but a minute ago he'd said something that had nothing to do with breakfast. Something about tea and trouble?

"Are we in trouble?" Sam asked.

"That depends," Nicolas answered. "Is it hunting season?"

Still braiding her hair, Jen answered, "No. Why?"

"I heard a gunshot."

"You're sure?" Jen said. Her fingers stilled on her half braid.

"Pretty sure," Nicolas confirmed.

Sam's pulse kicked into high gear at the mention of gunfire.

Knock it off, Sam told herself, but it was too late. Blood pumped through her veins so crazily, she could count each thump.

There's no reason for this, Sam thought, taking a deep breath.

Even though she'd always been a little afraid of guns, her own father had a rifle rack in his truck.

There were lots of harmless reasons for gunfire. Weren't there?

Sam tried really hard to think of one.

Nicolas didn't act worried. He doused the campfire and he couldn't have heard much past its hiss.

Sam chewed quietly as they ate a cold cereal breakfast topped with watery powdered milk. She paid attention to the sounds around her as she saddled Ace, but only heard birdsong and the rush of the small stream.

She was probably worrying for no reason, but she noticed Jen wasn't keeping up her usual chatter to Silly as she saddled her.

Nicolas only clucked his tongue as he fastened Lace's harness and backed her between the shafts of his cart. Sam had almost decided he'd forgotten the shots.

Then, he said, "I'll see you two back as far as civilization, then I'll be off."

Nicolas used a small fold-up shovel to turn the campfire ashes into the soil. He glanced around for anything he might have misplaced or left behind.

"Civilization means my house — River Bend Ranch," Sam said. "And that won't take you far off the main road."

If not for the gunshots, she might have told him not to bother riding the extra miles with them, because Nicolas was on a tight schedule.

Last night, he'd described his carefully planned journey. Sam had tried not to let her eyes glaze over from hearing all the details, but Jen had been so fascinated, Nicolas had retrieved his journal from the wagon.

"Is it written in code?" Jen had asked, peering over Nicolas's shoulder as he read his exact mileage to date.

"Not exactly." He'd laughed, then turned his journal so that Sam could see the squiggly marks interspersed with neat black printing. "It's shorthand. Before my parents' business took off, we lived in this teeny apartment and Mom had an old electric typewriter, a Gregg Shorthand chart, and a desk in a corner of the kitchen. She taught herself to be a secretary, but my sister and I learned shorthand and slipped each other notes no one else could decipher."

Since they were only children, Sam and Jen had told Nicolas how much they envied him, but he'd laughed. "That's because you don't know my sister."

Later, he'd shown them his camping permits, his backup plans for detours and delays, and explained how hard it would be on Lace if they encountered an autumn snowstorm.

Nicolas regretted spending two nights, instead of one, in this "mustang camp." He'd hoped they'd be far enough south to avoid harsh weather when it came.

Sam glanced skyward. Mounded like white cotton candy, the clouds didn't look threatening.

"I know my Gram will insist on feeding you," Sam told Nicolas, "so plan on staying for lunch."

"I don't know," Nicolas said. "I want to reach Darton tomorrow."

"You'll make up the time by not eating for the next two days," Jen told Nicolas. "Believe me, I'll be staying, too. Sam's grandmother is the best cook in the county."

"Well, maybe," Nicolas began.

"And Brynna should take a look at the colt," Jen said.

"Why?" Nicolas asked. Suddenly the line of suspicion above his left eyebrow was back. "Nothing's wrong with him."

Sam jumped in to explain. "It's just that Brynna — my stepmother — works for the BLM — "

"That would be, the Bureau of something?" Nicolas asked.

"The Bureau of Land Management, and — "

"I have all my paperwork," Nicolas broke in.

"Wait," Sam said. Why was Nicolas being so prickly? "The Bureau of Land Management is in charge of wild horses, not just land."

"Go on," Nicolas said after a few seconds.

"And Brynna is the manager of Willow Springs Wild Horse Center. She's a biologist and she wouldn't care about your paperwork unless you were doing something destructive — "

"Which you're not," Jen put in.

"Right," Sam said, "but Brynna is a wild horse expert. She might know what's up with your little tagalong."

Sam almost bit her tongue for sounding so cutesy, but the words had just come tumbling out as she tried to get Nicolas to settle down and trust her.

"I won't let anything bad happen to that colt," she added without thinking.

"Believe her," Jen said, slinging an arm around Sam's shoulders. "Ninety-nine point nine percent of the trouble Sam gets in is over wild horses. She loves them more than she loves her family and friends."

Jen gave a tragic sigh and let her head plop down on her friend's shoulder.

Sam rolled her eyes and Nicolas laughed, but then he said, "I've heard about the pens where they take wild horses they round up."

Sam followed Nicolas's gaze as he looked at the dun colt. Bored with all their talking, the colt had folded his legs and nodded into a nap.

"I know I can't keep him, but I wish he could stay free."

"Maybe that's not what he wants," Jen said, adjusting her glasses on the bridge of her nose. "After all, he joined up with you."

"He joined up with Lace," Nicolas corrected her. "He hasn't let me touch him."

Sam sighed. Each time she'd reached for the little dun, he'd skittered away, but she'd thought it was because he didn't know her.

"He could belong to someone," Sam suggested. "And Brynna knows how to look him over for brands, tattoos, microchips, and all that stuff."

"Something could have happened to his mother and he just wandered off on his own." Jen looked thoughtful for a moment. "Maybe his owner's posted a reward for—"

"I don't want a reward," Nicolas interrupted.

"Okay, we'll take it!" Jen said, but she shot a quick sideways glance at Nicolas.

"I don't want anyone to be suspicious," he explained. "I let him follow us because he wanted to, not because —"

"We're not suspicious and Brynna won't be, either," Sam said flatly. "We've had lots of experience with horse thieves —"

"Oh, good," Nicolas moaned.

" — and you're not one," Sam finished.

Nicolas fixed her with a look that said she couldn't possibly know that for sure, but Sam held up her hand.

"I know what I know," she insisted. Then she folded her arms and nodded.

"Forsters are notoriously stubborn," Jen pretended to whisper to Nicolas. "We might as well mount up and go. If you try to talk her out of it, we'll be here all day."

Minutes later, two riders, one caravan wagon, and a skipping foal trotted out into the autumn morning. The crunch and thud of hooves crossing orange and yellow leaves made their passage a celebration.

This was a lot better than lying in the dry grass waiting for vultures to swoop down for a peek, Sam thought, and she was pretty sure she didn't have any Sunday night homework.

When the horses settled into a walk, Nicolas took out his violin and played a jig he called traveling music.

Once, from the corner of her eye, Sam thought

she caught movement. She halted Ace and swung him around, backtracking in case the Phantom had followed, but she didn't spot the stallion.

Surely his instincts would keep him away during the daylight, no matter how much he liked Nicolas's songs. Especially if someone was firing a gun.

Sam reined Ace back onto the path. In a few steps he'd caught up with Silly and Jen.

They'd been on the trail for almost an hour when they heard another shot.

Sam and Jen drew rein. Lace snorted and stopped. She reached her chin over the colt's crest, pulling him close.

"Definitely a gunshot," Jen said.

"But what's that?" Nicolas asked.

Dry grass crackled as something crashed through it.

An animal, Sam thought. Was it fleeing the gunman?

"It's the coydog," Nicolas said.

Sam's breath caught. She twisted in the saddle and noticed Nicolas, sitting high on the wagon's driver's seat, had a better view. Could he really see—

The horses shied as a patchwork coat of coyote gray and white showed through the brush. The pup streaked closer, then sensed the horses and humans, and changed course.

Sam stood in her stirrups, searching for more swaying grasses that would show her that the female coyote and Blaze were with the pup, but she saw nothing.

The pup was doing okay on his own. Fleet and determined, he kept running. For a baby, he was doing a great job. He'd outdistance whatever followed him.

But why was he alone?

Chapter Seven ⌦

Cracking through the sunny morning came another gunshot. Then a yelp.

The dun colt bolted and Sam gathered her reins, ready to send Ace galloping after him until Nicolas shouted, "Let him go. He'll come back to Lace."

When she heard a volley of barks, Sam knew she couldn't have set off after the colt anyway.

"Blaze!" Sam screamed.

"Stay here," Jen ordered, but Sam didn't listen.

Galloping toward gunfire was a stupid thing to do, but she had to help Blaze. Shouting as she rode, Sam hoped whoever held that rifle would hear her human commotion and stop firing.

When she rode into the clearing, the damage was already done.

Sam's heart almost broke when she saw Blaze on his belly, ears back and mouth open in a submissive grin, begging the shooter to stop.

Her dog was alive, but his mate wasn't.

Blaze didn't notice she was there. His eyes watched Linc Slocum.

Mounted on his sturdy palomino, Linc held his rifle butt snug against his shoulder, but the barrel drooped. Done shooting, he wore a satisfied smile.

Hadn't he noticed the grieving Border collie pulling himself across the ground toward the coyote?

She was dead. Sam didn't have to look twice to know the female coyote would never move again. Sprawled so that her soft belly showed, with her shoulder wrenched to one side, Blaze's mate lay where the bullet had spun her back and killed her.

Nostrils flaring at the blood smell, Ace swung his head away, but stayed where Sam had stopped him. Silly gave a low, worried neigh. Hooves struck wood somewhere behind her, making Sam wonder if Lace was kicking at the cart. Maybe she wanted to run away and Nicolas wouldn't let her.

Blaze whined. *Poor sweet, smart dog,* Sam thought. Instead of attacking the armed man, he acted submissive. Blaze knew guns were loud. Maybe he sensed they were deadly, too, because his front paws dragged him closer to his mate, but he didn't growl.

Sam wasn't half as careful.

"What's wrong with you?" she shouted.

The smug grin slipped off Linc Slocum's face.

Jen said something. Nicolas did, too, but their voices were whispers next to the raging in her mind.

"Why do you have to kill things?" Sam yelled at Linc.

What if she rode straight at him, crashing Ace into Champ, knocking Linc to the ground so he'd know how it felt to be helpless?

The impulse evaporated as she stared at the black eye of the gun's barrel. She couldn't risk her horse. Or his.

A buzz like ten million killer bees droned in Sam's ears as she slid down from the saddle. Her knees didn't lock. She staggered a step before flinging her reins down, making sure Ace understood her order to stay ground-tied.

Blowing the horrible scents from his nostrils, the gelding stayed, but he didn't like it.

"That coyote attacked your dog!" Linc yelled defensively.

"No—" Sam began.

"She couldn't have. They were playing together last night," Jen snapped.

Jen had a lot to lose by confronting Linc Slocum, Sam thought. But she stood up for what was right.

Sam sank to the ground beside Blaze.

"Poor boy," she said. Her hands skimmed over his glossy fur. She saw no blood, but her fingers searched for hidden wounds.

Blaze lurched forward, crawling to the coyote's side, and Sam moved along with him.

A quick look showed a pink tongue hanging from the corner of the coyote's blood-flecked muzzle. Her teeth shone white. Her eyes stared brown and surprised.

Sam buried her face in Blaze's fur. She couldn't cry. She couldn't look weak when she stood up to Linc Slocum.

"I don't care what you say," Linc spoke in a lofty tone. "I was just plinkin' at coyotes and I saw that one"—he gestured with his gun barrel—"set on your dog. Savin' him was the neighborly thing to do."

"She was his mate." Nicolas's voice was quiet but bitter.

Sniffing, Sam looked at him. So did Jen and Linc.

For a second, Nicolas looked down at the reins in his hands, but then his chin lifted and he took them all in with a single look.

"It attacked your dog," Linc insisted. He jammed his rifle into his saddle scabbard, and cleared his throat.

When no one else spoke, he tried to shift their accusing stares away from him, to Nicolas. "I don't know who in heck you are. His 'mate'? You, with your fancy pony cart, you don't know nothin' about dogs and coyotes, tellin' a tall tale like that."

Lace couldn't have understood Linc's words, but she sensed their emotion. Her mighty front hooves lifted free of the earth. Her ears pressed back, disappearing into the thickness of her mane. Mouth opened wide, she threatened Linc with her teeth.

Nicolas drew back on the reins and murmured foreign, sweet-sounding words to her.

Sam felt a yell swelling her chest, but she tried to keep it from getting out by petting Blaze's head over and over again. He was panting now, uncomforted by her touch.

Without a chance to protect his family, his training had kicked in. Blaze knew he wasn't supposed to attack humans, but when his eyes rolled up to meet Sam's, they were filled with confusion.

She gave his head a final kiss and stood up. Before she uttered a word, Linc straightened in the saddle, trying to make himself taller.

"You jumped to a conclusion instead of seeing what was right in front of you," Sam said, doing her best to get through to him. "Jen's right. We saw Blaze and the coyote playing. You couldn't have mistaken that for an attack."

"They weren't playing," Linc said. "They heard me and took off running."

Pride filled his voice. Was Linc glad the animals feared him?

Sam swallowed hard. Fighting to keep her voice level, she must have made a faint sound Blaze took for a growl, because the dog scrambled to his feet. Lowering his head, he began to snarl.

Sam grabbed his collar. Linc deserved the punishment Blaze could inflict, but the man's hand hovered near the saddle scabbard, keeping his rifle within reach.

Linc hadn't snuffed out the coyote's life for food or because he was in danger. She didn't think he'd been afraid of the animal, either. Linc had killed the coyote simply because he could.

Linc stared at Nicolas, eyes darting from the brightly painted wagon to the beautiful horse. Then he shook his head. Sam didn't know what he was thinking, and she didn't care.

Jen urged her mare forward and looked down on the coyote. Last night, playing with her pup, the coyote's coat had shone like stardust. Not anymore.

"It was a clean shot," Jen said, but her voice quavered.

Sam could tell the words were all Jen could offer to comfort her, but they both knew they weren't enough.

"There, y'see?" Linc gloated. "I been plinkin' at coyotes since I moved here. I'm no beginner at gunplay." Linc puffed out his chest with pride. "Jennifer means she didn't suffer."

"I know what Jen means," Sam said. "But that coyote was just taking care of her family. You killed her for no reason."

Linc dismounted in a series of clumsy movements. He swung one heavy leg over Champ's back. His body wobbled, the saddle shifted, and his left stirrup creaked at the sudden weight before Linc made it to the ground.

"They're vermin," he said, slightly out of breath. "I'll skin this one out and hang its carcass on my barbed-wire fence to warn off the rest of his kind."

"Her," Nicolas said softly. He looked . . . not sick, exactly, but appalled. And interested.

Morbid fascination, Sam thought. Wasn't that the term people used when they didn't want to stare at something awful, but couldn't look away?

Even though he was a college guy, he lived in the city. He'd probably never seen anything like this.

"Are coyotes preying on your livestock?" Nicolas asked.

"Not that you got any right to interrogate me," Linc said, "but they could be. It's better to be safe than sorry."

Linc didn't keep track of ranch affairs. He left that to his foreman, Jen's dad.

Sam's quick side glance caught Jen shaking her head.

"There haven't been any calf kills by coyotes," Jen said.

Linc cleared his throat impatiently.

"If the sheriff hears about this—" Sam began.

"I'd have to pay a piddly little fine," Linc scoffed,

then he shook his head with pity, as if Sam just didn't understand. "I've got enough money to burn a wet mule, if you get my meaning. And I don't have to put up with accusations from a bunch of kids. I think I'll call the sheriff myself and tell him you all are trespassing on my land."

Sam didn't think they were, but the range was a patchwork of ranches and public lands. In these leafy woods, without landmarks, she couldn't be sure.

She didn't contradict Slocum, but she sure wanted to get to the sheriff first.

Nicolas had turned his attention back to Lace and Sam could see why. The mare's black-and-white tail swished with edgy energy. She launched a backward kick that struck the wagon, and Nicolas murmured to her.

"Who is that kid, anyway?" Linc aimed his question toward Jen. "And what kind of jibber-jabber is he talking?"

"I couldn't say," Jen told him, and Sam shrugged.

"I don't like his looks," Linc told them, as if Nicolas couldn't hear. Then he called out, "That's some horse."

"Thank you," Nicolas said.

"Where'd you get her?"

"She was a gift," Nicolas said.

Linc snorted, then focused on Nicolas's frayed jeans and dark skin before he said, "Yeah, I bet."

Sam wished Gram were here. Gram said you

should try to love everyone, but Linc Slocum made that impossible. With three words and a look, he'd accused Nicolas of being a liar and a thief.

"Come, Blaze," Sam said. She patted her leg, trying to attract the dog's attention before he noticed Linc had squatted next to the coyote's body.

She didn't know what Slocum had in mind, but the fur bristled on Blaze's back.

She'd better get Blaze out of there, Sam thought.

"Let's go," Jen said, backing Silly alongside Ace. She looked down at Blaze. "He'll come with us, won't he?"

"I hope so," Sam said, then hesitated. "Don't you think we should stick around and hope the colt comes back? And"—she lowered her voice to a whisper— "what about the pup?"

"Stick around? I told you," Linc said, "you're trespassing and you can by God expect a visit from the sheriff."

Linc looked annoyed that she didn't tremble at his threat.

"The sooner we get away from this spot, the sooner the colt will return to Lace. This is what scared him," Nicolas said. He lifted his chin in a gesture that included the clearing, Slocum, and his gun.

"Okay," Sam said. "He'll probably catch up."

As they moved off, she glanced back and saw Linc pick up the coyote. Her limp body looked nothing like the light, dancing creature from last night.

She flopped like a rag in his hands.

Sam turned her attention to the trail leading home.

"Good boy, Blaze," she said.

The Border collie walked so near Ace's front hooves, the gelding could have stepped on him.

Sam tried to be cheered by each stride Ace took away from the clearing, but dark thoughts followed her.

Linc Slocum was worse than careless and big-headed.

She'd seen him holding the lifeless bodies of two mother animals—first a cougar and now the coyote. Both had left young behind. The young cougar had turned dangerous. She didn't know what would become of the coydog.

She did know that Sheriff Ballard and Phineas Preston, the retired police officer engaged to Mrs. Allen, didn't trust Linc. Both lawmen were working to connect him with a ring of horse rustlers.

Shooting this coyote would be more evidence that Linc was a criminal, Sam thought. The minute they rode over the bridge to River Bend Ranch, she'd tell Dad, Gram, Brynna, and anyone else who'd listen what had happened. Then she'd call Sheriff Ballard. And Preston. She'd keep telling people until she stopped Linc Slocum.

He won't get away with it this time, Sam vowed. *I won't let him.*

Chapter Eight ∾

Sam drew in a breath of yellow leaves and damp tree bark.

They'd progressed in silence for about twenty minutes, all eager to leave Slocum behind.

Sam gave Ace's warm bay neck a pat. Her movement caught Blaze's eyes. Sam clucked her tongue at the dog and told him "Good boy" once more.

The Border collie whined. Was he favoring his right side?

Holding her breath, Sam watched the dog keep pace with Ace and Silly. He glanced over his shoulder at a tinkling sound from Nicolas's wagon, then trotted on.

Blaze looked all right. And she'd felt him all over

for injuries, but what if she'd missed something? Linc had admitted he'd shot after the animals as they ran. Had one of his bullets grazed her dog?

"Is he limping?" Nicolas called out over the sound of wagon wheels.

"Maybe," Sam said, flashing Nicolas a grateful look. Blaze wasn't his dog, but he was concerned. "I was just watching him."

"He can ride in the wagon," Nicolas offered. "There's room in the back, or up here beside me."

Sam darted a quick look at Jen to see if her opinion of Nicolas was rising, too, but Jen looked like she was in a world of her own, staring at the trail ahead.

"Thanks, but I don't think he'd do it," Sam said. "Blaze is really suspicious of moving vehicles."

"That's sensible," Nicolas said.

"I don't know," Sam said, watching Blaze as he sniffed through some trailside brush. "Even if he was really hurting, I bet he wouldn't let me wrestle him up into your wagon. He won't get in my dad's truck without a fight."

"Do you know how much I hate Champ belonging to him?" Jen blurted.

"Yes," Sam said. So it seemed that Jen couldn't get the image of Linc's palomino out of her mind. Sam explained Jen's apparent tangent to Nicolas, telling him how Jen's family's ranch and palomino breeding farm had failed and Linc Slocum had appeared out of nowhere to rescue them with an offer to buy the

ranch and let her family remain in the foreman's
house.

"According to my maps, this is public land we're
traveling over," Nicolas said, reminding them of
Linc's threat to report them as trespassers.

"Not all of it," Jen said, and for some reason, she
suddenly looked brighter. "This area's been resur-
veyed recently and there were all kinds of mistakes in
the old maps."

"So that's what Linc was talking about," Sam
said. "Brynna's been studying maps lately, too."

Her stepmother had been staying up late and getting up early to analyze maps rolled out to cover the
kitchen table. The BLM and local ranchers were
revising boundaries, and it was Brynna's job to
puzzle out how the new border lines would effect
Nevada's wild horses.

"Why do you look like that's a good thing?" Sam
asked Jen.

"Can you guys keep a secret?" Jen asked, lowering her voice.

"Sure," Sam said.

"Yes," Nicolas answered, looking surprised.

"Last year, remember, right after your dad and
Brynna's wedding, how my mom and I went to visit
relatives in Utah?" Jen asked.

"Yeah," Sam said slowly.

Jen and her mom had left for the holidays and her
dad had remained behind, because Jen's parents had

been fighting. Big time. People who knew them had feared they were on the brink of a divorce. Why would memories of that time bring a sparkle to Jen's eyes?

"Mom was mad when we left," Jen explained, "and she took along some money of her own that she'd been investing since before she and Dad got married."

"But—" Sam interrupted.

"It wasn't enough to save the ranch," Jen said. "In fact, her investments didn't start doing well until last year, but she was thinking of buying a house up there."

A house? Sam shuddered. No wonder Jen had been so cranky and depressed during Dad and Brynna's wedding.

"But she didn't do it. Did she?" Sam asked.

"No, but what she did do was something that would have made Dad insane if he'd known," Jen told her.

"Should I be hearing this?" Nicolas wondered aloud. He shifted on the driver's seat of the wagon and both girls laughed at his discomfort.

"Who would you tell?" Jen asked sensibly. Then, she went on, "One of Mom's cousins was working for a small newspaper, and got a chance to buy it, but she needed help. Financial help. So Mom loaned her some money."

Jen covered her mouth at her mother's daring

and Sam could see why. Ranchers depended on nature and other unpredictable factors from season to season. That was a big enough risk without loaning a relative thousands of dollars.

"So, your mom's kind of a gambler," Sam joked. Maybe the thought was more amusing because it was a break from brooding over Slocum, or maybe Jen's excitement was contagious.

"In a good way, it turns out, because . . ." Jen drew out the suspense, then finished, "A national chain of newspapers wants to buy my cousin's newspaper and they've offered her a million dollars for it."

Nicolas chuckled, but Sam could hardly catch her breath.

"It's in the hands of lawyers right now," Jen said airily. "But when we get our share—"

Sam couldn't smother her delighted shriek. When Ace flattened his ears in irritation, she simply leaned forward and kissed his mane.

"Nothing's settled," Jen cautioned, but her smile stayed in place.

"Still," Sam said. "Wow."

That explained why Jen had confronted Linc Slocum so fearlessly. Maybe the Kenworthys could stop depending on Linc Slocum for their house and every penny they spent on food, clothes, and horses.

"Would you leave"—Nicolas gestured at the countryside—"this?"

"No way," Jen said. "We'd buy back our ranch.

At least part of it. We hope. Then we'd get our Fire and Ice palomino breeding program up and running again and, best of all, we'd get out from under that monster's thumb."

Sam took one hand from her reins and jabbed a celebrating fist skyward. She didn't think Ace would put up with a round of applause.

Jen sighed. Relief from telling the secret made her sink a bit in the saddle.

"Will Linc sell?" Sam asked gently.

Jen held up crossed fingers, but Sam's brain had already swerved away from reality to start tallying possibilities.

"If Linc gets in trouble for shooting the coyote, his offenses against the wild horses might resurface, and if someone digs up the shady real estate deals out of his past—remember, the ones you told me about, Jen? You said someone actually committed suicide over the scam Linc pulled?" Sam asked.

"Yeah, I remember," Jen said.

"And then," Sam said, "if he went to court as part of the horse-theft ring—"

Sam broke off. Maybe all those things couldn't come together in the same trial, but wouldn't a judge hearing even half of that just be itching to send Slocum to jail? And with Linc Slocum jailed, the Gold Dust Ranch—

"Sam, stop," Jen said. "You're about to chew a hole through your lip."

"I am not," Sam said, but she touched a knuckle to her bottom lip. It was already sore because she'd been biting it as she concentrated. "Still, if there's any justice—"

"There's always that big *if*," Jen said.

"We've got to hurry and tell Sheriff Ballard what Linc did before he reports us—"

"I don't think you have any reason to worry," Nicolas broke in. "Or hurry."

Sam had almost forgotten he was there, but she turned to listen.

After all, Nicolas was a college student, and as an outsider, he might be in a better position to observe.

"Did we miss something?" Sam asked.

"There's a saying attributed to Napoleon," Nicolas began.

"Who conquered most of the civilized world of his time," Jen said to Sam.

With a wave of her hand, Sam brushed away Jen's explanation. She had heard of Napoleon.

Sam twisted in the saddle to face Nicolas and said, "Tell me."

"It's something like, 'Never interrupt your enemy while he's making a mistake.'" Nicolas paused to let the words sink in and both girls smiled.

"I love that," Jen said.

"Me too, and Linc's always making mistakes," Sam said.

"Let him make this one," Nicolas suggested.

"Don't race to report him. That way he'll be making himself look bad, by admitting to the sheriff that he shot the coyote. Then you two can step up as concerned citizens who just happened to have witnessed his crime."

"What are you studying in college?" Jen asked Nicolas.

"Pre-law," Nicolas confessed. He shrugged as if he didn't want them to think he was showing off. "My grandfather claims he's never met a gypsy lawyer, though I'm sure he's wrong."

"Perfect," Jen said, with a contented sigh. "I'm glad you're on our side."

Chapter Nine ❧

$\mathcal{L}$ace kept calling for the dun colt.

Every few minutes, Sam heard the vardo's wheels crunch to a stop. Then, after a moment spent sniffing the air and listening, the mare would cast her neigh out in another direction.

The colt must have heard the plaintive sound, but maybe he was too frightened to return, or perhaps he'd lost his way.

As Sam, Jen, and Nicolas drew closer to River Bend Ranch, wind scuttled leaves ahead of them. Yesterday's summery mood faded.

Tomorrow was a school holiday. Nevada Day,

they called it, in honor of the day Nevada had been admitted to the United States. No matter how often their parents and teachers told them otherwise, lots of Nevada children thought their day off, which usually coincided with Halloween, had been declared so that they could recover from a late night of candy and excitement.

Sam was glad tomorrow was a holiday. She'd have time to begin her campaign to see that Slocum got what he deserved.

But after Nevada Day came Thanksgiving, then Christmas, and though the excitement of holidays and a new baby lay ahead, she also felt melancholy. There'd be fewer days to ride and, most likely, she'd see the Phantom far less once he and his herd holed up in their hidden valley for the winter.

Wait a minute, Sam thought. In her mental list of holidays, she'd missed something. Nevada Day and Halloween, Thanksgiving, then wasn't there another holiday? Schools didn't get a break on Columbus Day, so that meant . . .

"I missed Jake's birthday!" Sam gasped suddenly.

"By like a month," Jen said.

"Who's Jake?" Nicolas asked, but Sam barely heard him.

Jen's words reminded Sam of her own birthday party. When Jake had said the big box full of film for her camera wasn't what he wanted to give her, but it had been the only thing he could think of, Jen had been her usual sarcastic self, wondering aloud where Sam had gotten the idea she could have a birthday every year.

She'd known Jake all her life, and though they didn't make a huge deal of each other's birthdays, they always gave each other something. When Jake had been recovering from the horseback accident that had broken his leg, she'd given him a beautiful leather headstall for Witch and a book about Native American trackers. Even when they'd been little kids, she'd given him a bunch of carrots for his pony.

This was the first time she'd completely forgotten.

But why hadn't someone reminded her? Like Gram. Or Jen. Sam reined in her impulse to blame someone else. That wouldn't help, and besides, she was fourteen years old. She knew how to use a calendar.

"I didn't even give him a card!" Sam mumbled. "How stupid can I be?"

"Don't panic, Sam," Jen said.

"Hey, if I'd missed your birthday—"

"I would have reminded you with merciless harassment."

"Exactly. But Jake just let it go," Sam moaned.

"He might not even have noticed," Jen said.

Yeah, right, Sam thought.

"Who's Jake?" Nicolas asked again.

The breath Sam drew to tell him puffed right back out of her as Ace's sudden stop jerked her forward against the saddle horn.

Her bay gelding threw his head so high, she couldn't gaze through the frame of his ears in the direction he was staring. He gave a shrill neigh. Then, as he bobbed his head, and his black mane slapped his neck, Sam saw the dark figure riding their way.

"*That's* Jake," Sam said, pointing.

Sam wondered if there was a name for this weird feeling of guilt mixed with relief.

Probably not. Most people who were glad to see a friend hadn't forgotten his birthday for an entire month.

Just the same, Sam was glad to see Jake. She just wished he'd shown up sooner.

Not that she, Jen, and Nicolas hadn't handled Slocum just fine. She hadn't collapsed into tears or smothered the rich rancher with his own huge hat, although the image of Slocum's pudgy legs kicking in protest was kind of satisfying.

Sam shook the picture from her wicked imagination.

She'd done fine, but if Jake had been riding beside her, Slocum might have apologized instead of threatening to report her to the sheriff. Jake had a more calming effect on people than she did.

Sam heard the gentle thud of hooves and saw Jake sway in the saddle, moving with his horse as if they were a single creature.

A centaur, she thought, one of those mythological beasts that were half horse and half human. And if she rode every day for the rest of her life, no one would ever mistake her for one.

"How did he get so close without any of us noticing him?" Nicolas asked.

"It's what he does," Jen said sourly.

Sam smiled. It was strange that even though he rode Witch, a big black mare, Ace hadn't noticed Jake until he was a quarter-mile away.

"I hope he's a friend of yours," Nicolas said, "because he's got the colt with him."

Just then, the dun colt, which had been running in Witch's shadow, pranced on ahead of her. Jake kept Witch at an easy lope as they followed. The black mare hovered behind the colt without hurrying him.

"What you're seeing is typical Jake," Jen told Nicolas. "He has this totally annoying habit of showing up at the right place at the right time."

"It's only because he's the best tracker in the state, not because he's psychic or anything," Sam explained.

"A tracker?" Nicolas asked. "Like a bounty hunter?"

Jen gave a short laugh. "Maybe that's a career choice he should consider."

Sam wondered if her two best friends' competition would last their entire lives. Probably.

"No, but where we'd just ride on past a patch of dirt, he looks down and reads it as if someone had scratched out a five-paragraph essay with a sharp stick," Sam explained.

"I get it." Nicolas stared toward the black horse and dark rider with surprised appreciation. "That's something I should learn before my next journey. It would be useful, being out in the wilderness like I am. I haven't had any bad experiences, but I could know what was"—Nicolas made a circular motion with his hand—"going on. I've been surprised a time or two and if I'd known the signs to look for, I might not have been."

Nicolas broke off with a short laugh. "Sorry, I was just sort of thinking out loud. I mean, a tracker probably wouldn't have been startled when a sheepherder and his flock showed up at his campsite. I didn't know they were coming until the guy shouted hello."

"You knew we were coming," Sam said.

"Sending two horses on ahead provided kind of a big hint," Nicolas said.

"You sound like you're going to do this again," Jen said.

"I might," Nicolas said, then shrugged. "A lot depends on how things go between here and Sacramento."

Sam saw Nicolas rub his wrist. Was it sore, or was he thinking of a watch and the time he'd waste riding to River Bend Ranch?

With a loud snort, Witch gave in to Jake's order to walk as the colt ran for the big paint mare.

The staccato hammering of small hooves made Sam swallow hard. The little guy was so glad to be back where he belonged. Lace obviously felt the same way. She tossed her mane with such enthusiasm, it sounded like a flag flapping on a windy day.

"Go ahead, girl," Nicolas said.

He slackened the reins so Lace could trot forward to meet the colt. Even though he wasn't hers, the mare greeted the little dun with a nicker that tugged at Sam's heart and made her push away the reminder that it was almost time to wean her filly Tempest.

Jake hung back until the colt and mare quieted.

Was he tipping his head forward that way on purpose? Did he know his face was shadowed by his black Stetson?

He had to be curious about Nicolas, his beautiful horse, and the unusual wagon, but Jake only touched the brim of his hat in greeting and waited for someone else to say something.

"Thanks for bringing the colt back," Nicolas said and when Jake just shrugged, Nicolas held out his hand. "I'm Nicolas Raykov."

Jake rode close enough to shake hands.

"Jake Ely," he said, accepting Nicolas's handclasp.

Sam glanced at Jen. Nicolas had been a little standoffish with them, and he sure hadn't been friendly with Slocum, but he seemed different with Jake.

Jake didn't return Nicolas's smile and Sam hoped Nicolas understood it only meant Jake was shy. He had friends, but most days when she saw him on campus or in the hallways of Darton High, Jake stood at the edge of a circle of guffawing guys, with a quiet grin lifting one corner of his mouth.

As Nicolas and Jake's handshake broke, they both looked away. Sam caught Jake's eyes darting between the girls and Nicolas. Was he wondering how she and Jen had ended up riding home with a stranger?

Sam was set to tell Jake about the coydog, Slocum's trigger-happy killing, and everything else, but for some reason she put it off a few more minutes.

"Nicolas is driving from Seattle to Sacramento," she said.

"Yeah?" Jake asked.

Nicolas gave a proud nod.

"That wagon he's driving is known as a vardo," Jen explained, "and the mare is a Gypsy Vanner horse. There are fewer than a hundred of them in the entire country, but he was lucky enough that she was imported especially for him by his grandparents, because he's a gypsy."

"Naw, really?" Jake said with a straight face. "I took him for a Comanche."

Sam heard Jen's sound of strangled frustration, but it didn't bother Sam. This was the way it went between her two best friends.

"He's doing this to further appreciate his roots," Jen said, denying Jake time enough to gloat.

"Plus, my grandparents thought it was a good way to break up my relationship with my girlfriend," Nicolas said. "They don't like me mingling with non-gypsies and she's 'not one of us,'" he confided.

Sam met Jen's eyes. Why hadn't Nicolas mentioned this part of his journey's purpose? Was he sort of telling Jake he had no interest in Sam or Jen, in case Jake did?

Sam felt her cheeks heat with a blush. Nicolas was way off base if that was what he thought. He could probably tell that, though, by the way Jake just sat there instead of firing off a bunch of questions.

Nicolas's eyes crinkled at the corner, enjoying the situation for some reason Sam didn't understand, and when Jake said, "Hope you're not lettin' them guide you somewhere," Nicolas took it as a joke.

"No, I'm just seeing them home," Nicolas said, then gave Jake a short version of how they'd met where the wild horses watered.

Sam noticed Nicolas was nice enough to leave out the saga of the exploding biscuits. She also noticed Jake's quick glance up the trail, the way he turned his head a fraction of an inch to take in the hillside, then the ridge, near Cowkiller Caldera.

To Sam, Jake's quick survey of the area said he knew exactly where they'd been.

For sure, he'd followed their tracks. Maybe he'd

seen the coydog's prints, too, Sam thought, and suddenly she saw no point in keeping this meeting sweet and social.

"Did you meet up with Linc Slocum?" Sam asked.

"Detoured around him. Saw . . ." Jake paused. His voice deepened, as he finished, "where he'd been."

That simply, Jake let Sam know he'd figured out the whole awful story.

"Jake, I hate him so much," Sam blurted. Something in the way he kept his feelings closed in always made Sam spill hers.

Jake met her eyes, held them, and then nodded.

"She had a pup," Nicolas said.

"Yeah," Jake acknowledged.

"But Jake, it's Blaze's pup," Sam said. "He's a coydog."

For once, she'd surprised Jake so completely, he showed it.

Disbelief made Jake's jaw drop, then snap closed. He frowned and took in a breath, then said, "Guess you're sure."

"He has part of a white ruff, just like Blaze," Sam said, touching the back of her own neck. "And last night all three of them were playing together."

"Hmph," Jake said.

As Jake sat thinking, Sam saw Nicolas glance toward the sun. It was directly overhead.

"Hey," she said to him. "If you want to go ahead the way you had scheduled, you don't have to drive home with us."

"Oh, nice, Sam," Jen said. "First you bribe the guy with your Gram's cooking. Then, once you've got his taste buds tingling, you tell him to forget it."

"You know I didn't mean—"

"Doesn't your Gram make home-fried chicken or steak on Sundays?" Jake teased.

"And pies," Jen put in. "Didn't Sam say her grandmother's up every Sunday morning before church rolling out piecrusts?"

"No, I didn't," Sam said, pretending to pout. "Sometimes she makes chocolate cake."

"A few more hours probably won't throw me completely off my timetable," Nicolas said, but then flattened ears, an angry squeal, and a single lashing kick erupted from Witch.

"Oh, for . . . ," Jake muttered.

Then, even though Jake probably didn't feel like "lecturing" his horse, he reined the cranky mare away from Jen's palomino, Ace, the amazed Gypsy Vanner, and the dun colt.

Sam watched as Jake reminded Witch she couldn't get away with bad manners. Jake never lost his temper with his horse. He simply made the mare behave.

Usually Jake's cues to his horse were invisible, but he worked her hard, now, backing her in a long straight line, then making her spin left and stop. Then right, and stop. Finally, he galloped her through flying lead changes, weaving around invisible barrels. At last, he let the black mare come high-stepping back to the rest of them.

Sam was about to applaud when Silly—who still couldn't believe Witch didn't want to be her friend—extended her palomino muzzle in a second greeting.

"Silly, keep your nose to yourself," Jen scolded.

How could Jake have known—from his position on her back—that Witch bared her teeth, ever so slightly, at the palomino? He must have sensed it, because he drew in a breath and the black mare stiffened. For a few seconds, Witch didn't move. Then, she swung her head around to look at her rider.

Jake didn't return her look. He sat loose and balanced in the saddle, reins resting in his left hand while he whispered a low and tuneless whistle.

Finally, Witch stamped a front hoof and stared past Silly as if she weren't there.

Lace's teeth chattered against her snaffle bit.

"I don't know whether she's terrified or applauding," Nicolas joked.

"Lace is a good girl," Sam said. "She has nothing to worry about."

Just then, Ace tossed his head to get rid of a fly, and they laughed at his seeming agreement.

Their good moods lingered as they rode toward River Bend Ranch. Even when the thought popped into Sam's mind that Linc Slocum could be calling the sheriff right then, she held to Nicolas's theory that when your enemy makes a mistake, it was the best you could hope for.

Sam kept her reins in her steady left hand and crossed the fingers of the right hand that hung free as she rode. With any luck at all, Sheriff Ballard would see this entire situation the same way she did.

Chapter Ten ⁊

"He shot Blaze's mate and he didn't even say he was sorry," Sam told her dad. "And he kept his hand on his rifle like he might have to use it."

"On who?" Dad interrupted.

Sam took a breath.

They stood just outside River Bend Ranch's round corral. Moos and snorts came from three restless steers inside the pen and she'd just introduced Nicolas to Dad and Dallas, the ranch foreman.

Dad had grabbed onto one detail in her description of what had happened in the clearing with Linc Slocum and he looked angry.

She couldn't help seeing Dad as Nicolas might.

Wyatt Forster was a man of medium height and

weight, but the leather chinks and sweat-streaked shirt he wore while schooling his new horse to work with cattle made him look kind of tough.

Not mean or unfriendly, though. In fact, Dad had dismounted and led Blue outside the round corral as soon as he'd sighted the vardo and the three young riders.

Dad had been holding Blue's reins in his left hand and loosening the fingertips of his right deerskin glove by tugging at them with his teeth when Sam's words sunk in.

Dad always had the solid look of a man who worked hard, but as he drew up, straightening each vertebra and squaring his shoulders, he looked like a man who didn't take kindly to someone threatening his daughter.

"I've had just about enough of this," Dad muttered to Dallas when Sam didn't answer right away.

Dallas bumped up the brim of his hat and asked Sam, "The unlucky cuss didn't actually pull his gun on you, did he?"

"No, but—"

"He had his hand on his rifle," Dad repeated.

Ace nudged Sam. Her horse was eager to be stripped out of his tack and released into the ten-acre pasture, but she petted his neck while she replayed the scene with Slocum in her memory. She didn't want Dad to overreact to this one detail since she had worse information to tell him.

"I couldn't read his mind, and I don't even want to," she said, "but we were the only ones there—just me, Jen, Nicolas, Blaze, and the horses. The coyote was already dead when we got there and we saw him jam his rifle back in his scabbard." The picture of the female coyote, with her blood-flecked muzzle and lolling tongue floated back to the surface of Sam's memory. "I don't think he could have been afraid she'd get back up, but he kept his hand on his gun."

Dad's face darkened to a deep red, but he didn't say anything more about Linc. He turned his attention to Jen and Jake. Both straightened in their saddles.

"Since you two are still mounted up, could I ask you to let those steers out and haze 'em back across the bridge? I think me and Blue are finished with that sorta work today."

Dad patted Blue's damp neck. The Spanish Mustang was colored in the pearly shades of the inside of a seashell, and though he had to be weary, he watched the other horses with interest.

"Sure," Jake said. He reined Witch over to the fence and unlatched the round pen's gate so quickly, Sam thought he was trying to escape. Jen was right beside him.

Jen and Jake moved the cattle as easily as if Dad had asked them to bring him a glass of water, but Dallas's question brought Jen up short.

"You having coyote problems over at your place?" Dallas asked.

"No." Jen's eyes followed Jake, but she held her palomino in place for a few seconds.

"Didn't think so," Dallas said. "Grace—that's Samantha's grandma," Dallas said, aside, to Nicolas, "has been sayin' she hasn't seen many rabbits in her garden this year. That means the coyotes are eatin' small prey, not calves and such."

"My dad says Linc's never gonna get the idea that 'you don't interfere with somethin' that's not botherin' you none.'"

Jen had mimicked Jed to perfection, and she took Dad's and Dallas's smiles as permission to catch up with Jake and ease the cattle onto the bridge over the La Charla River, and on toward the open range.

Sam liked the saying Jen had attributed to her dad, and she agreed that Linc didn't know how to leave well enough alone. In fact, she'd just thought of another example of it.

"Not only that; he halfway accused Nicolas of stealing Lace."

As soon as she uttered the words, Sam could tell Nicolas wished she hadn't.

"Is that so?" Dad asked Nicolas.

"I don't need his approval or anyone else's," Nicolas said. "All I need is my horse."

Dad narrowed his eyes and rubbed the back of his neck. He shaded his eyes to watch the old blue truck rumble across the bridge, after the cattle had crossed, but Sam saw Dad's disapproval.

He didn't say anything wrong, Sam thought, but by the way they all stared at the blue truck pulling up at the ranch, she knew she wasn't the only one feeling uneasy.

Pepper braked to a stop, got out, and walked to the truck bed. He'd just returned from Phil's Fill-Up in Alkali, judging by the gunnysacks of chicken feed each of his arms were curled around. They had to be heavy, but he sidetracked from going straight to the barn when he set his eyes on Lace.

"I'll see to her, if you like," Pepper said, setting down the feed.

Pepper had only looked this smitten once before. Then, he'd been looking at the actress Violette Lee. In Sam's opinion, Lace deserved his attention about a hundred times more.

"Thanks, but I'll take care of her," Nicolas said. "We're only stopping for a little while."

Although Sam had encouraged Nicolas to drive on, before, now she wanted him to stay. He and Dad had gotten off on the wrong foot. For some reason, she wanted them both to have the chance to change that.

"Don't go," Sam said. "Gram will be here in a minute, and then we'll eat."

Nicolas looked down as if fascinated by the reins in his hands. His face flushed as red as Dad's had just a minute ago.

"Really, I should be going."

"You're welcome to stay." Dad's invitation had a hint of apology in it. Nicolas looked up and his eyebrow didn't quirk in skepticism.

"It's my understandin' there'll be chicken-fried steak, mashed potatoes, and peach pie with vanilla ice cream," Dad added.

Nicolas gave a disbelieving chuckle, then accepted Dad's invitation with a nod.

"You can take your wagon 'round back of the barn and leave it. Then, unharness your horse, maybe bring her back up here for some water, if you like."

"Thank you," Nicolas said, then smiled at Pepper, who showed no sign of moving away from the big mare.

"She's sure a good-lookin' horse," Pepper said.

As he moved closer, the dun colt ducked behind the wagon, but Lace was as drawn to Pepper as he was to her. Pressing her face against the young cowboy's chest, the Gypsy Vanner inhaled his scent as if recognizing an old friend. Next, she rubbed her forehead against his collar bone with such enthusiasm, he stumbled back a step.

"She's like a big dog," Pepper said. "She's a little heavy for a cow horse, but once you got a rope on a steer, I don't think he'd be goin' anywhere."

For an instant, his eyes left Lace and flicked to Dallas, but when Lace widened her exploration to tug the hem of his shirt free of his jeans, Pepper laughed and forgot about the other people.

Pepper had to reach high to do it, but he scratched Lace's crest and the mare's white-lashed eyelids drooped with pleasure.

"And, hey, we have the same color hair in places," he said.

As he lifted the white strip of Lace's mane, Sam wondered why she hadn't noticed its pinkish tips before.

"What's that?" Sam asked, since it clearly wasn't natural.

"Chili powder," Nicolas said. "The colt kept chewing on her mane and she wouldn't make him stop. So I had to. He was pulling out big hunks of it. See how that part's shorter? So, I made up a watery chili powder solution and combed it through her mane. The next time he took a nip, he didn't like it so much."

"She throw that colt?" Pepper asked Nicolas.

"No, he's an orphan she took on," Nicolas said. "You want him?"

No one took him seriously, but Sam thought Nicolas might really be looking for a good home for the tagalong colt, since he was worried about its safety.

"Blue sure seems to have taken a shine to him," Dallas chuckled as the Spanish Mustang pulled to the end of his reins to touch noses with the dun colt.

"Look at them," Dad said. His tone was low as Blue sniffed the colt's long forelock, then the black mark that crossed the dorsal stripe at his withers.

The colt stood statue-still, out of respect for Blue, until Nicolas clucked for Lace to listen up. When he drove her in the direction of the barn, the colt looked torn. Should he stay with Blue or follow his surrogate mother?

He pawed up a clump of dirt and for the first time, Sam really studied the colt. His color reminded her of a crumpled brown paper bag smoothed out, with black lines showing where it had been creased. His spine, shoulders, and knees showed some of those lines, faint as if they'd been inked on with a fountain pen. His face might have some thread-thin lines, too, but the colt didn't give her long to look. With a teeter-totter buck, he ran after Lace.

Sam was so busy watching him and wondering how the colt had ended up alone that she missed the change in conversation until Dad drew her back into it.

"So, you're convinced the coyote Linc missed is actually Blaze's whelp?" Dad asked as the Border collie walked away from them and crawled into his favorite den, the space under the bunkhouse step.

"Yes," Sam said. "Should we go after him?"

"I don't know about that," Dad said, looking startled.

Oh no.

Sam busied herself with Ace's cinch. She had to look away from Dad.

Pulling the end of the cinch loose, she tugged

upward until the tongue of the buckle flopped free and Ace sighed.

I don't know about that. Couldn't Dad see they had to ride out with Blaze, find his son, and bring him back to River Bend? Dad looked as if she'd suggested something bizarre.

"I don't know a whole lot about coydogs," Dad admitted. "Brynna might. Or someone at the university. I'm thinking it's a bad mix. Could inherit a coyote's dislike of humans without their fear, since his daddy's a dog. Besides, we've got one good dog."

Sam bit the inside of her cheek to keep from talking back. This wasn't the time to squabble with Dad, but she knew a ranch could use more than one watchdog. As for the coydog's attitude, she'd work with the pup, helping him become as alert and faithful as his father.

Sam had the feeling Jen and Jake might have backed her up on this, but when she looked around for them, it was clear they wouldn't be much help.

Jen and Jake sat their horses, way across the ranch yard, pretending they were guarding the bridge against the steers' return. They weren't, though. Sam knew they felt the uneasiness quaking between her and Dad and they wanted to stay out of range.

But her friends weren't quite uncomfortable enough to ride on home, Sam thought with a mocking smile. Nope, they knew it was about time for Gram and Brynna to come home from church. They were determined to stay for lunch, and they hadn't even heard about the peach pie yet.

As Sam watched, Jen took off her cream-colored Stetson and twirled it on one finger. That looked like a small celebration and it could only mean they'd spotted the Forsters' only car coming this way.

Yep. Sam heard the hum of the yellow Buick, and Jen and Jake were backing their horses away from the bridge.

Gram had barely parked the car when Brynna slid out of the passenger's seat and started toward Dad.

Brynna wore an electric-blue maternity sundress that showed off her tanned arms and legs. Sam thought she saw her stepmother stuffing half of a candy bar into a patch pocket shaped like a white daisy.

"You'll never guess who was in church," Brynna said. "It's a wonder we weren't all killed by a bolt from above."

"Now Brynna," Gram said, laughing in a way that clearly supported her daughter-in-law's sarcasm instead of discouraging it.

"Couldn't have been Slocum," Dallas said. "He was out shooting coyotes."

Brynna frowned and Gram flashed Dallas a scolding look before she hustled past toward the kitchen.

"Dinner'll be in twenty minutes," she snapped.

Brynna's mood might have been a little restrained by Dallas's comment, but she still slung both arms around Dad's neck and gave him a hug.

"I'm all sweaty," he protested.

"I noticed," Brynna said, kissing his cheek. "I just don't care."

"I'm gonna leave you two lovebirds alone," Dallas said. He shook his head before moving off. "And I'll look Blaze over if he'll let me."

"Me too," Sam said. Sometimes she wondered if Brynna got all mushy with Dad so that other people would get embarrassed and give them some privacy.

"No," Brynna said, "don't go, Sam. You'll want to hear this. Well, actually you won't want to, but—" Brynna gave a deep sigh. "You need to."

Then it had to be about wild horses, Sam thought. Brynna didn't believe in hiding the hard facts of mustang management from her stepdaughter, no matter how unpleasant they were.

"Spit it out," Dad said. "You're worryin' me."

"I knew he was coming," Brynna said to Dad. "I just didn't know it would be this soon."

"Aw, shoot," Dad said. He swept his hat off and slapped it against his chinks. "Already?"

Dad seemed to know exactly which "he" Brynna was talking about, but Sam didn't.

"Who's here?" Sam asked.

Brynna reached up and tightened the ponytail

that took the place of her sensible weekday French braid.

"Norman White will substitute as manager of BLM's Willow Springs Wild Horse Center while I'm on maternity leave," Brynna said. "And for some reason, he's shown up early."

"At church?" Sam squeaked.

"Right in the middle of the front row," Brynna confirmed.

He's not as evil as Linc Slocum, Sam thought. Still, Norman White was known by BLM colleagues as "No Way Norman." He was so cautious in spending the bureau's money, he was the last person Sam wanted filling in for her horse-loving stepmother.

"But you're not going on leave until December, are you?" Sam asked.

"No, of course not," Brynna said. "I feel great and I'll work until the very last minute. Nothing would make me happier than going into labor right there among the wild horse corrals. It would give him less time to mess things up."

Dad's mouth opened. The emotion telegraphing down the reins to Blue made the Spanish Mustang jerk back and roll his eyes. Dad's expression said he was about to ask Brynna to tone down her statement.

But when Brynna whirled toward Dad with her hands on her hips, he didn't say a word. And neither did Sam.

Chapter Eleven ∽

Even to Sam, Brynna's declaration sounded a little crazy. But Brynna hadn't exactly been herself lately. Forgetful, uncoordinated, and—though she'd gained exactly the right amount of weight according to her doctor—embarrassed by her craving for sweets, Brynna was still devoted to the wild horses and she fought hard to prove that to everyone.

Just the same, Sam knew Brynna wouldn't do anything to endanger the baby. Something about Norman White's early arrival had her stepmother worried.

Sam had first met Norman White before Brynna and Dad were married. He had filled in as manager of Willow Springs while Brynna was on a business trip to Washington, D.C., and he'd ordered the death of a dozen "unadoptable" wild horses.

Sam had heard about the mustangs' death sentence through Dr. Scott, a young vet who hated the idea of putting down healthy horses, and Sam had persuaded Mrs. Allen, their neighbor to the east, to go with her to just look at the doomed mustangs.

The horses had included Faith, a blind Medicine Hat filly, and her mother, plus other mustangs Norman White thought were too old or ugly to find homes. Sam had always wanted to ask him if he wondered what would happen to him when he grew old, lost his hair, and maybe had trouble moving around.

Luckily, Mrs. Allen's heart had gone out to the condemned horses. They'd been the start of her Blind Faith Mustang Sanctuary.

Now, Brynna smooched at Blue, and the wary mustang flicked his ears in her direction. Although he didn't leave his place beside Dad, he shifted his weight forward and extended his muzzle far enough that when Brynna reached her hand out, they touched. Their greeting made Dad smile.

"Why is Mr. White here so early?" Sam asked.

"To investigate some irregularities in my office procedures." Brynna pronounced the words in a prissy way.

"Oh, B.," Dad said, using his nickname for her as he gave her shoulders a squeeze.

"I'm not worried about it," Brynna said. She

leaned against Dad so that he left his arm around her shoulders and looked up to tell him, "I've always followed policy to the letter."

"So which 'irregularities' could he be talking about?" Dad asked.

"He wouldn't discuss that at church," Brynna said, "but—and I know this sounds paranoid—I got the distinct feeling he'd only come because he knew I'd be there."

Sam believed Brynna. If Brynna thought Norman White was spying on her, he probably was.

Dad nodded. He believed her, too, but he offered another explanation.

"C'mon now," Dad said. "Even old No Way Norman's allowed to have a yen for church, isn't he?"

"Sure," Brynna said, "but once I spotted him sitting up front, I couldn't keep my eyes off him. I had a hard time paying attention to my own devotions, because I could see him writing something."

"Writing? Like taking notes?" Sam asked.

"Like that," Brynna admitted, "but when the service ended and we were all filing out, he dropped what he'd been working on and, well, I was right behind him." Brynna touched the rounded front of her dress and laughed. "Norman was pretty surprised that I managed to bend down quick enough to swoop them up and return them to him."

"What was it?" Sam asked.

"A couple things. I didn't get a good look at the

diagram, but I saw the computer spread sheet had dollar signs and the names of different herd management areas. I have no idea what he's scheming to do while I'm gone." Brynna's tone verged on despair.

Ace mouthed his snaffle loudly, then swung his head against the reins. Sam followed his glance toward the hitching rail nearest the house. Jen and Jake were tying their horses. Sam couldn't blame Ace for reminding her that she'd already loosened his cinch. That usually meant he was done for the day.

"This doesn't sound like good news, but you've got almost a month to keep your eye on him, right?" Sam asked, and when Brynna agreed, Sam added, "I'd better go put Ace up."

Brynna nodded, then pointed to Sam's saddlebags and bedroll.

"Hey! I didn't even ask how your camping and vulture-watching went."

"It was great," Sam said.

Then, Sam heard the clopping of heavy hooves, which meant Nicolas was leading Lace this way for water, and she yearned to talk about something that wasn't serious. Homecoming week at school, maybe, or a spur-of-the-moment Halloween party. She wished she and her friends could just take a picnic lunch somewhere else, away from River Bend Ranch and its problems.

Dad looked at his dirty, horsehair-covered hands and said, "Better wash up and turn Blue out."

When Brynna just nodded, Dad said, "We can talk more."

Sam led Ace toward the pasture, then shouted back over her shoulder, "And we have company for lunch."

Brynna was usually cheered up by visitors.

Sam freed Ace. As she hurried back toward the house, she saw Dad was still talking with Brynna. He hadn't gone to wash up or turn Blue out at all. Were they discussing something they didn't want her to hear?

Dad's head jerked up, and he said, "Besides, you're gonna like Sam's new friend."

"I bet I will," Brynna said.

Sam thought it probably revealed something significant about her social life that Brynna started glancing around the ranch yard at animal level. As if her stepdaughter couldn't have a new human friend.

"He's a kid with a horse and wagon. A real gypsy, isn't he, Sam?" Dad asked and there was something too hearty and totally un-Dad-like about the way he said it. "Sam?"

"Uh, yeah," she said. "His name is Nicolas. Jen and I met him on the trail."

Brynna frowned.

"He's a college student, but he and his family are gypsies, from England," Sam explained. "He's the first Raykov—I think that's how you pronounce his last name—born in the U.S., and he's taking this journey to kind of live the life of his ancestors for a semester," Sam told Brynna.

"That sounds interesting," Brynna said, but her vague tone contradicted her words.

"Jake likes him," Sam offered. She'd learned that unfair as it was, Jake's opinion counted for more, with Dad and Brynna, than hers did.

"Is that him?" Brynna asked.

It was. Nicolas came around the corner of the barn and Lace followed, though she wore no halter and he held no lead rope. On playful hooves, the dun colt came with them.

"That's Nicolas and his horse Lace. She's a Gypsy Vanner. They're really rare and he's driving, if you can believe it, all the way from Seattle to Sacramento. He's carrying everything he needs for his six-month trip in his wagon. It's called a vardo. Jen and I—"

"Is there an unusual marking on that colt's forehead?" Brynna interrupted.

"No. . . ."

"He looks a little skittish. Can you get close enough to pet him?"

What was going on with Brynna? Sam wondered. The colt was cute, but Lace was amazing. And rare.

"Sam, have you peeked under his forelock?"

"No, he's—"

"Wild?" Brynna finished for her.

"Not exactly," Sam said, though she felt a flash of understanding. Part of Brynna's job was making sure mustangs weren't taken from the wild by anyone except the federal government.

"Samantha, tell the truth," Brynna insisted. "Does your friend own that colt?"

Sam stared across the ranch yard, trying to remember everything Nicolas had said about the dun colt. She watched Nicolas stroke Lace's black-and-white shoulder as she drank, but she was remembering the way the dun colt had tried to join the Phantom's herd.

"He said it was a stray," Dad cut in, casting an impatient look at Sam. "A leppie foal that started tagging along with the mare."

"Where did he join them?" Brynna asked.

"I think he told me," Sam admitted. "It was somewhere I'd heard of, but I can't remember. We can ask him, you know." Then, when Brynna looked like Sam had been sassy, Sam added, "Can't you tell me what you're worried about?"

Brynna parted her lips to speak, but then shook her head.

"Not ten minutes ago he was offering that colt to Pepper," Dad said. Sam could tell he was trying to coax the truth from Brynna, too. "He says he can't take the young one along with him travelin' the highway."

Tempest, Sam's own black filly, called to the dun colt.

They must be about the same age, Sam thought, and when the little dun ran a bucking loop around Lace, Sam wished she could turn this baby out to play with Tempest.

"I'm probably being too suspicious," Brynna stated, "but if I'm right, it's going to mean trouble. Sam, why did you have to bring that boy and his horses here at all?"

That didn't sound like Brynna. She was always sociable and welcoming to everyone.

"What is wrong?" Sam managed.

"If that colt's the horse I think he is, Norman White will recognize him. The herd of Spanish Mustangs that Blue came from has turned out to be genetically significant in a university study, and the adopters of the other horses have become pretty loud in accusing BLM of losing—or selling off—the last remaining stallion from the herd."

"But that didn't happen," Sam said.

The BLM hadn't known Blue's herd was almost pure Spanish, descended from the horses conquistadors brought to the New World centuries ago, when the herd was rounded up. The BLM had declared the horses' territory too sparsely vegetated to sustain them through winter.

How could people accuse the BLM of losing or

selling off the last remaining stallion when he—Blue—and his yearling colt had been gelded and adopted?

"You told me one of the mares from that Good Thunder Meadows bunch died," Dad said slowly. "And when you got interested in the bloodlines, because of Blue, your boss put you in charge of tracking down her missing foal . . ." Dad's voice faded as he stared at the dun colt and shook his head.

"Do you think that's him?" Sam asked.

"Honey, that's a terrible long shot," Dad told Brynna, but suddenly Sam knew it wasn't.

Dad had researched the place Blue had come from. Good Thunder Meadows had earned its name because an ex-cavalryman had lived in that high mountain valley and when a severe winter left his Indian neighbors hungry, he'd used his rifle to bring down game for food. They'd named the sound of his rifle "good thunder."

Now, Sam remembered the glow of firelight on Nicolas's face as he'd told her and Jen that the foal had showed up in the area of Good Thunder Meadows.

"Don't you think it would look pretty fishy if I'm investigating the colt's disappearance and he ends up here?" Brynna asked. "This is not a good time for me to be in possession of stolen government property. Norman's certainly read the description. He'll recognize the colt just like I did."

"That's not going to happen," Dad said sooth-ingly. "At least not right away."

"It might, since your mother"—Brynna wore a wry smile as she tapped Dad's chest with her index finger—"asked Norman White over for lunch. He'll be here any minute."

Chapter Twelve ❧

If Nicolas felt three pairs of eyes watching him as he stood beside Lace at the water trough, he didn't show it. He sang to his horse, soothing her with the same melody he'd used in the forest the night before. Even though the darkness and trees had given way to a sunlit ranch, the words gave Sam chills.

"Gypsy gold does not clink and glitter, oh no," Nicolas's voice soared, even without the violin to guide it. "It gleams in the sun and neighs in the dark, ah yes."

"His voice." Brynna uttered the words in awe.

"The tune reminds me of that old song," Dad said, and silently snapped his fingers as if the gesture would bring the title to mind. And it did. "'Oh

Shenandoah,' is that what it's called?"

"It has that same lonely quality," Brynna said, but she used a dismissive tone. When she glanced toward the bridge over the La Charla River and the highway beyond it, Sam knew her stepmother's attitude wasn't linked to Nicolas's song. "But right now, before we have more company, I need to have a look at that colt's forehead. The one that got away had a distinctive marking."

Sam didn't know how they were going to do this without making Nicolas feel like he was suspected of something, but somehow Brynna managed.

Maybe her big belly and bouncy ponytail didn't look threatening, Sam thought. And maybe Nicolas would have reacted differently if Brynna had been wearing her uniform, but she wasn't. After admiring Lace and Nicolas's ambitious trek down the West Coast, she told him the little dun might be the orphan colt of a Spanish Mustang mare from a desolate area near the Oregon border.

"It sounds like him," Nicolas said. "He fell in with us around Good Thunder Meadows. At least, that's what the sheepherder called it. It wasn't on any of my maps."

"I wonder if you can bring him close enough that I can check his brow," Brynna said. "He was described as a dun with a marking like two upside-down *V*s, one inside the other, where you might expect to see a star."

"That's it," Nicolas said. "It's a lot like the markings on his knee. They look like they were done in fountain pen, and then got rained on."

Brynna smiled at the description, but then Nicolas's brows rose and his jaw dropped slightly. "Described by who?" Nicolas asked with a fleeting breathlessness. "If he belonged to someone and escaped, why is he so wild?"

"He was probably born wild," Brynna said. "He was brought in with the rest of the Good Thunder Meadows mustangs by the Bureau of Land Management. Now we know he's a valuable little horse, but then . . ." Brynna shrugged. "He got separated from the rest somehow."

"And his mom died, you said," Nicolas repeated. "So, sure, I can trot Lace around, he'll follow, and his forelock will blow back. You can take a look, but what happens to him after you're sure?"

"I have to think about that," Brynna said.

Nicolas's eyebrow quirked up skeptically and his lips flattened into a line.

Gram picked that moment to shove open the squeaky screen door.

"Dinner will be on the table in five min—" She must have been in a hurry, because the door slammed before they heard the rest, but no one doubted the meal was on its way.

If Nicolas had wanted to avoid giving Brynna time to identify the colt, he could have taken the chance right then, but he didn't.

"We'll hurry," Nicolas said.

Without a halter or a lead, he began jogging next to Lace. Tossing her head up in high spirits, she walked beside him and Sam could tell Nicolas would have to pick up the pace if the huge mare was going to trot.

"Come on, slowpoke," Nicolas teased the mare.

Lace dipped her head, then flung it high. Her mane tossed in variegated glory, and Lace lifted her knees to pursue her master.

"*She's* his, that's for sure," Brynna said quietly, and then the dun colt kicked up his heels and ran after the big mare.

His black scrap of forelock lifted on the wind and there on his brow were the two black shapes, pointing upward like twin arrowheads.

"Yep," Dad said finally.

"Thanks!" Brynna shouted, and Nicolas's pace slowed immediately. "He looks a little muddled by all this."

"Nicolas or the colt?" Sam asked.

"The boy, of course," Brynna said.

"Now what?" Dad asked.

Brynna's answer was to motion Nicolas toward the house, so Sam guessed Brynna wasn't about to blame the colt's disappearance on him.

"Now lunch," Brynna said to Dad. "I'm starving, and if Norman White is much later, I might just eat his pie and mine, too."

Then she strode toward the house, and only Sam saw her dip into her daisy-shaped pocket, pull out a candy bar, and finish it off before reaching the kitchen.

Six chairs were arranged around the oval mahogany table. As usual, for Sunday lunch—which Gram called dinner—Sam had been asked to set the table with candles and cloth napkins. It made a pretty setting, but Gram gave Nicolas less than a minute to express admiration and thank her before pointing out his seat and asking him to take it.

During the meal, Brynna kept everyone's focus off Nicolas, as if his declaration that he wanted to leave the colt behind moved him beyond suspicion.

At least as far as Brynna was concerned, Sam thought, but would Norman White be so easily convinced? If he ever got here. It was rude that he hadn't called to say he wasn't coming, and it didn't fit with his attention to detail.

Sam was glad he hadn't shown up, but his absence put off the discussion between him and Brynna about the colt's future. The little dun couldn't be returned to Good Thunder Meadows alone.

"They must be awfully rare," Gram said, snagging Sam's attention back to the dinner-table conversation. "Brynna, what sort of natures do coydogs have?"

Brynna held up a finger, signaling she had to

finish chewing before she could answer, but Jen stated an opinion to fill the gap.

"I've read that coyotes are raised by both parents," Jen said, pushing her glasses up her nose. "And I don't see how Blaze could have been doing his part."

"Hey," Sam jumped in to defend her dog. "How could he? Every time he wandered away, we went looking for him."

"I'm not blaming him," Jen said. "And he was treating the coydog like his puppy."

"Jen's right. The males usually have a big part in raising the pups," Brynna said finally. "That's probably one reason coydogs are unusual." She broke off then, frowning. "Has anyone looked Blaze over? Made certain he wasn't injured?"

"Sam did," Jen said. "I saw her palpating him—" Jen flashed a condescending look at Jake. "That means examining him with her hands."

"Thanks, doc," Jake said. He winked before forking a bite of chicken-fried steak into his mouth and trading amused glances with Nicolas.

"Anyway," Brynna went on, "there should have been more than the one pup."

Dad shook his head slowly. "Still some around here who believe in denning."

"What's that?" Sam asked.

"Never mind," Gram said, casting a worried look at Brynna.

Sam didn't insist on an answer. She had heard of people putting dynamite or poison in coyote dens and she was afraid it was something like that. Her imagination didn't need more awful details to process.

"Now, you boys," Gram said, "let me get you seconds on mashed potatoes. You, too, Jennifer. Heaven knows you could use a little meat on your bones."

"Isn't she great, Nicolas?" Jen asked in a dreamy tone.

"Absolutely," Nicolas said, then he leaned toward Sam. "She's exactly like my grandmother."

"How old was he?" Brynna asked. "The coydog?"

Sam, Jen, and Nicolas looked at each other, at a loss even to guess.

"Probably less than a year," Sam said.

"That's about right," Brynna said, nodding. "Although, I'm going largely on what I know of coyotes. The parents start bringing the pups solid food at about a month, and they're usually weaned around nine weeks. They leave their dens and run around with their parents, learning to hunt and hide, at about this time of year."

Once more, Sam thought of all the nights they'd stood on the front porch, calling for Blaze. Had he felt torn between his ranch family and the one in the wild?

"How long do they stay together?" Jen asked.

"Until autumn," Brynna said. "About now they kind of split up for the winter."

"So," Nicolas said sensibly, "sad as it is, having the young one on his own now isn't"—he searched for a word—"unnatural?"

"Not at all," Brynna said. "He'll probably come through the winter all right."

The conversation veered away from the coydog before anyone suggested a future for him, but Sam thought Jake looked far more thoughtful, moving his fork through the last of his gravy, than the task really warranted.

"Okay, I'm going to do it," Brynna said after Gram had ordered her to sit quietly while Sam cleared the table.

Watching everyone else troop outside into the blue and gold afternoon to learn more about Gypsy Vanner horses might have made Sam cranky, if she hadn't made a plan. She'd already figured out Dad's feelings about bringing the coydog to civilization, but he'd deferred to Brynna's expertise, before she'd gotten home.

Now, all Sam had to do was get Brynna on her side.

"See that you do," Gram said to Brynna, as Sam handed her the neatly stacked plates, ready to slip into the sudsy dishwater.

"Actually, I was talking about Norman White, not sitting quietly." She smiled at Gram as if she should have known. "If I don't keep him in the loop, I can't expect him to take appropriate actions. And by appropriate, I mean doing things the way I would," Brynna admitted. She took a quick breath then, and winced in a way Sam had come to know as her reaction to the baby kicking. "It's still early, but it's possible I could go into labor any time, so I've got to make sure Norman and I agree on a few things, now."

In the quiet that followed, Sam looked over to see Brynna leaning her chin into her palm, thinking.

"After all," Brynna said, "I must have scared him off, somehow. Otherwise, he would've come for lunch."

"I'd say his rudeness matches what you told me about his accommodations." Gram turned both handles, hot and cold, on full blast into the sink.

"It wasn't worth taking a stand over," Brynna said.

"His accommodations? Where's he staying?" Sam asked.

"In my office."

Gram made a quietly disapproving noise.

"He's staying there? Like sleeping there, too?" Sam demanded.

"That's how it sounds," Brynna said.

That was more than pushy, Sam thought. It was creepy. And Brynna had said he'd brought BLM papers and the wild horses with him to church. That had to mean he was going through Brynna's files. He probably had a right to do that, but couldn't he wait until he'd taken over Brynna's job?

"I don't like it, either," Brynna said to Sam and Gram. "Just the same, I'll phone him, so there's no question about everything being aboveboard. Not that it isn't," Brynna hurried to add. "I believe every word Nicolas said about the colt, and the fact that he's willing to leave him behind speaks for itself." Brynna drained her glass of milk. "But Norman White is dedicated to the bureau above everything else."

"Except maybe his own ambition," Gram muttered.

Sam knew what that meant.

Over the last few months, Norman White had been a self-appointed campaigner for the federal government's new program, which required the BLM to sell horses over ten years old—like Blue—or young horses that hadn't been adopted after three tries—to the highest bidder.

Usually, the highest bidder was a slaughter-buyer like Baldy Harris of Dagdown Packing Company, which processed horses into meat.

So far, Brynna had managed to turn down every offer on technicalities, but Sam knew her refusal to go along with the new plan had been noticed. Brynna was running out of excuses, and Norman White wouldn't bother.

He praised the sell-not-adopt program as an efficient way for the bureau to make back money it had spent protecting mustangs.

"Samantha, you look like you're sucking a lemon," Gram pointed out.

"Worse than that, huh, honey?" Brynna asked.

Sam nodded and released a deep sigh.

"Still, I'd better tell him what's going on so that Nicolas doesn't get implicated in something dirty. If I know Linc Slocum, he's already found a way to turn this into something else."

"He did say we were trespassing," Sam said.

"That's nonsense," Gram muttered, but then Sam could tell she made an effort to rinse the dishes more quietly.

She and Gram listened while Brynna dialed her own office and talked to Norman White in a way that was downright pleasant. Reciting the alpha angle identification mark from Blue, she asked Norman to check her files for the detailed description of the missing colt.

"Um-hm," Brynna said, and when she held a pen poised above a pad of yellow paper without writing anything down, Sam knew Brynna had gotten everything right, from memory. "Yes, I do. It is, a real coinci—" Brynna stopped and Sam turned in time to see alarm in her stepmother's eyes. "Really. So my call was forwarded to your cell phone and—are you all right? Young stallions can be unpredictable and one of our local ranchers was feeding horses at the roadside not long ago, luring—" Brynna broke off her list of excuses, but Sam couldn't figure out what else was going on. "Oh, Norm, that's not necessary. Of course, you're still welcome to stop by. The colt, however, isn't a major issue for us."

Brynna listened in silence for a while, then said, "If you insist. It sounds like you're about ten min— Yes, right over the La Charla River. Sure. We'll be watching for you."

"Now, he's decided to drive out here?" Gram guessed.

"Oh yeah," Brynna said. "And his attitude hasn't been improved by the fact that he had to swerve off the road to miss two wild horses."

"What did they look like?" Sam asked.

"They were both brown," Brynna repeated in a flat tone. Then, holding her head in her hands with both elbows resting on the mahogany table, she mimicked Norman White, "'Says here that you adopted an animal from that exotic herd yourself. That's a mighty interesting coincidence. I think I'll come out there and see that everything's as it should be.'"

"That creep," Sam snapped.

"That's not the best part," Brynna said, looking up at Sam. "I'm to detain Nicolas until Norman gets here, or 'he'll know the reason why.'"

"He can't tell you what to do!" Sam said, then put down the dish she was drying for fear her tight fists would shatter it.

Just then, there was a knock at the door and all three of them looked at each other. Unless Norman

White had magical powers, it couldn't be him.

"Come in," Gram called. "Dallas? What's wrong?" she asked as the old foreman opened the kitchen door.

Dallas whipped his battered hat off his silver hair, nodded toward Gram, then looked at Brynna.

"Ma'am, you might want to come out here and take a look at Blaze. That dog won't let me check under his right foreleg. He's pantin' like a lizard on a hot rock, but when I fill up his water dish, he ignores it. Truth is, I'm afraid he got creased with one of Slocum's bullets, after all."

Chapter Thirteen ꙮ

Sam hurried outside behind Brynna as a formation of geese flew honking over River Bend Ranch, not in their usual strict *V* but in tatters that looked more like part of a *W*. It seemed like a bad omen to Sam, and she wondered if she was just feeling guilty.

"Has Wyatt had a look at him?" Brynna asked as she followed Dallas.

"No, ma'am, everyone's over admirin' that Gypsy horse, and that's fine with me. I don't think this dog needs a lot of noise and hoopla."

Dallas stopped next to the bunkhouse step. Sam heard Blaze panting in the dark, cool space beneath it.

"I really did check him over," Sam told Brynna.

"Your dad told me there was a lot going on, with

Linc killing things and accusing people of who knows what," Brynna said.

"Still, I did," Sam insisted. She bit her lip hard enough that she felt a jolt of pain to match Blaze's.

"Let's just see what we can do to help him," Brynna said. "Here, boy."

Brynna squatted in front of the step, using both hands to keep her balance while she crooned to the dog.

"Come here, sweet dog," Sam joined in, and she heard Blaze's tail thump in pleasure.

"That's about all he does," Dallas said. "He was out here, and then when I noticed he was limping and tried to take a look at him, he slipped loose and hid."

"It's probably nothing major," Brynna said. "I'm sure Wyatt would have noticed if it were."

"I know what to do," Sam said. She flopped full-length in front of the step and dragged her palms over the dirt in front of her. "Crawl, Blaze, crawl!" Sam looked aside at Brynna for a second. "Dad hates him knowing tricks, but I taught him some."

Blaze whimpered, but he slowly obeyed.

"Maybe that's not such a good idea," Sam said.

"It will probably hurt him less than dragging him out by his front paws," Brynna said. Then, as the dog emerged and rolled onto one side, she said, "Excellent dog. Let's have a look."

Sam held Blaze's head and Dallas steadied his body while Brynna examined the Border collie. Gram brought a first-aid kit from the barn and when Dad saw her, he strode after her.

"I've by golly had enough of Linc Slocum," Dad said. He watched Brynna use first aid scissors to snip away Blaze's shiny fur so she could study the wound. "How bad is it?"

"Just a nick." Brynna's voice was muffled as she bent to her work.

"From a bullet," Sam said.

"Maybe," Brynna said.

"Linc admitted he was shooting at them as they ran. That's why I think we should call the sheriff," Sam said.

Brynna's concentration broke. Her eyes lifted to look at Sam, then Dad, before she kept working.

"It's not illegal, honey," Dad said.

"Shooting dogs?" Sam demanded.

"Shooting coyotes," Dad clarified.

"How can that not be illegal?" Sam asked, but when neither Brynna nor Dad spoke up, she had a feeling she was the one who was wrong.

But she'd sworn not to let Linc Slocum get away with this. What should she do next?

"I'm guessing this is from a bullet," Brynna said, "but we won't know for sure unless there's a little piece of metal the bullet left behind."

"I'm giving that man a piece of my mind," Gram said. "What was he thinking? Shooting where there were kids and horses."

"He didn't see us until we broke out of the woods," Sam admitted.

"And right there," Dad insisted, "is where Ballard's gonna get 'im. You've got to know who and what's around you before you go firing your weapon."

Drawn by the sight of Sam, Dallas, Brynna, and Dad crouched over the Border collie, everyone but Nicolas left Lace and the dun colt to come see what was going on.

No sooner had they gathered around the worried dog, though, than the BLM truck driven by Norman White bumped across the bridge.

"I'm outta here," Dallas said.

"Can you finish up alone?" Dad asked Brynna as he, too, began to walk away.

"*Brock, brock,*" Brynna said, imitating a chicken, but Dad and Dallas didn't laugh or slow down.

"I'll go help Nicolas," Jake said.

"Well, don't help him too far away from here," Brynna said, placing a small pad over Blaze's wound, then unrolling a bandage to wrap around his body and hold it in place. "Mr. White's come to talk to him."

Jake went still. He stood, thinking, then asked, "Slocum call him about trespassin'?"

"Maybe," Brynna said. She wobbled as she tried to stand up, and Jake cupped his hand under her elbow.

There was something so considerate about the gesture, it made Sam blink. She'd have to stop thinking about Jake as a kid, because he was acting like a man.

"Thanks, Jake," Brynna said, and Jake looked away as if she'd swatted him.

A shy man, Sam thought, grinning until Brynna continued talking.

"Mr. White is mainly here because I told him I thought the little dun was a BLM horse that went astray. And Norman had to come see for himself."

But he's not a BLM horse, Sam thought. The colt was wild. His mother might have died in captivity, but the colt deserved his freedom.

Sam stared toward Lace, Nicolas, and the colt and imagined she saw brush strokes of black branching over his coat. Those marks were the symbol of ancient horses, the kinds of horses painted on cave walls. His kind had survived in a hidden valley, just as the Phantom's herd had.

Would he have been accepted into the Phantom's herd, instead of driven away, if the honey-colored horse were still the Phantom's lead mare?

That's not even worth thinking about, Sam told herself.

Phineas Preston, Mrs. Allen's fiancé, a former police lieutenant, loved the mare. She might have been the Phantom's lead mare, but before that she'd been Cha Cha Marengo, Mr. Preston's police horse. If he had anything to say about it—and he'd be sure he did—she'd never run wild again.

And in this one way, the Phantom was no different from other herd stallions. He needed a lead mare to keep order while he fought off challengers for his band. If his attention was divided between his herd and another stallion, he'd likely lose battles, then his family of mares and foals.

"Thanks for sticking around," Brynna told Sam, as Blaze trotted after the cowboys. Then, lowering her voice to a faint whisper, she said, "I know you don't like him, either."

"Not a bit," Sam agreed, and then, when Jen walked toward them from the barn, practically dragging her feet, Sam added, "Have you noticed it's just us girls?"

Her voice must have carried to Jen, because her best friend wound each of her braids into coils that looked like cinnamon rolls and said, "Have you noticed I smell like I spent the last two nights sleeping in the dirt? Oh yeah, that's right. I did."

"I'm glad you're here, Jennifer," Brynna said.

"I only stayed for the mashed potatoes," Jen joked, but she tilted her head to one side, watching Norman White approach.

"I remember him from that day when we herded the horses back to Mrs. Allen's ranch," Jen said. "He struts like a little general, doesn't he?"

Norman White wore the same style of khaki uniform Brynna put on for work, but Brynna just looked pressed and pulled together. Norman White's military air—with his shoulders back, chest out, and chin high—matched his short-cropped crew cut. Still, he was no taller than Sam.

Humming something under his breath, Norman walked toward them.

Sam wasn't very good at "Name That Tune" games. Even though she'd heard the song—kind of a march—before, she turned to Jen and whispered, "What's he humming?"

Brynna raised her eyebrows in Jen's direction, too.

"Darth Vader's theme?"

Sam smothered her laugh into a snort, but Brynna broke into laughter. She tried to cover it by clearing her throat, then coughing.

"Nice to see you again, Mrs. Forster," Norman said. "It's not a bad drive out here, though it's clear excess horses are going to have to be gathered for public safety. I had to pull off the road to avoid those two I mentioned and some brush scraped the truck."

"It probably didn't go through the paint to the metal," Jen observed. "I bet you can just rub out the scratches."

"Have we met?" Norman asked.

"Jennifer Kenworthy of the Gold Dust Ranch," she said, reaching way past halfway to meet his handshake.

Norman nodded, then glanced at Sam. "And

you're the stepdaughter."

Afraid anything she said would sound sarcastic, Sam just nodded and brushed off the front of her shirt, which was still dusty from lying on her belly to talk to Blaze when he was under the porch.

"About the colt," Norman said, turning back to Brynna. "I'm sure you're right, there's nothing to worry about, but I'd rather be safe than sorry."

Jen gave Sam a gentle elbow in the ribs, but Sam had already realized that both Norman White and Linc Slocum had used the same expression to cover another motive altogether.

Linc hadn't shot the coyote to be safe. Norman White hadn't driven to River Bend Ranch to see if Nicolas, a twenty-year-old college student, was some kind of threat. Both men were busy showing everyone who was boss.

Norman insisted on checking out the dun colt before he met Nicolas. Walking around with a printout attached to a clipboard, he studied the colt as it tried to hide behind Lace. Check marks were placed with such broad movements, no one doubted the man who'd be Brynna's substitute had agreed with her assessment that this was the missing colt from the Good Thunder Meadows herd.

When Brynna introduced Nicolas to Norman White, the man inclined his head as if he were royalty and Nicolas was a peasant. Nicolas pushed his black hair away from his forehead, and the focused intensity in his expression reminded Sam that Nicolas planned to be a lawyer.

"Norm," Brynna said, interrupting their analysis of each other, "the colt mothered up with Nicolas's mare, and clearly it's the one that went missing from Good Thunder Meadows. Even at a glance, you can see he fits with the other grullas and duns from that area."

"Clearly," Norman said.

"Now we need to backtrack, find out what happened between the capture point at Good Thunder Meadows and the truck that took the horses to the adoption point."

"That's pretty clear, too," Norman said with a look at Nicolas that could only be called a leer.

"No, it's not," Brynna said. "No one mentioned theft until a possible suspect appeared."

It took Sam a few seconds to understand Brynna's response to Norman's hint that Nicolas had stolen the colt from the capture site.

"You must admit it's pretty suspicious that this drifter just showed up with the most valuable—and portable—member of the herd," Norman said.

Sam couldn't believe Norman White was talking this way in front of Nicolas. And how could Nicolas tolerate it in silence?

"But if he stole the colt, why would he turn up here at my ranch?" Brynna asked.

"Mrs. Forster," Norman said in an embarrassed

tone, "you'll have to answer that."

Sam recoiled. She couldn't believe he really thought they were trafficking in stolen horses. It made her angry, but Brynna refused to be baited into an argument.

"Come on now, Norman, remind yourself of what we thought before Nicolas showed up. We were pretty sure that the BLM misplaced the horse, right?"

"Well, yes," Norman admitted. "Still, this issue deserves more study. Let's load the colt into my truck and I'll drive him up to Willow Springs where he can't go missing again."

"Since this case is still mine to study and I haul horses all the time, how about if I bring the colt up to Willow Springs on Tuesday, after tomorrow's Nevada Day holiday," Brynna suggested.

Norman looked dubious, but before he could accept Brynna's suggestion, Nicolas interrupted.

"Excuse me." Nicolas's smooth tone startled the bureaucrat.

"Yes?" he said.

"Mr. White, what can I do to put your mind at rest before I get on my way?"

Wow, Sam thought, when Nicolas became a lawyer, that voice would come in handy. It was not only charming, but soothing.

"You can leave the colt behind." He said it like a dare.

"Fine," Nicolas agreed.

Norman White exhaled loudly. "But your departure isn't imminent."

Norman must have seen the flash of defiance in
Nicolas's eyes, because he added, "I want you to stay
here for a few days until we can establish how you
came into possession of the colt."

Nicolas folded his arms and, for the first time,
Sam noticed his shirt. White with billowing sleeves, it
looked like something a pirate—or a traditional
gypsy—would wear. Nicolas drew a patient breath,
then explained, "The colt followed my mare, and
tagged along with us for a few weeks. Even if I
stayed, I could tell you no more than that."

Norman White set his jaw in what was supposed
to be a tough look. "You'll need to stay."

Sam chewed her lip. She knew Brynna had some
law-enforcement authority. Did Norman?

Apparently Nicolas wasn't about to ask.

"I hope you'll forgive me," Nicolas said, moving
back toward the barn, "but I'm on a tight schedule
and I'd like to put a couple hours in on the road
before dark."

He clapped his hands and Lace pulled the vardo
around the corner of the barn. The gypsy cart glowed
green, red, and gold in the afternoon sunlight.
Jogging alongside was Witch, carrying Jake.

Jake had said he was going to help Nicolas. It
seemed they'd decided the best thing they could do
was plan a confident departure. Sam wanted to ride

along with them, but she'd already unsaddled Ace.

She stifled her sigh of disappointment as Nicolas gave a small shrug and gestured toward his brightly painted vardo.

"If we let him go, you'll bring the colt to work with you on Tuesday. Is that right?" Norman asked Brynna. "You'll stake your reputation and the reputation of this ranch on that?"

"Of course," Brynna said. With her hands on her hips, she gave a short-tempered nod.

If Nicolas had been paying attention to the BLM managers' irritated exchange, he didn't show it.

"As you can see, Mr. White, if you need me, I'll be quite easy to find," Nicolas said as he hopped up into the driver's seat and lifted the reins. Even that move seemed choreographed, as the leather strands draped like ribbons to Lace's bit.

Nicolas should be paying attention to Brynna, Sam thought. Without spelling out her trust in him, Brynna was still showing she believed Nicolas.

Eyes wandering from Nicolas to the rider beside him, Norman White asked Jake, "You're one of those Ely boys, aren't you?"

Jake just touched the brim of his hat.

When it was clear his bluster had no effect on Nicolas or Jake, Norman said, "All right, then, as long as the colt stays behind."

"He's staying," Nicolas assured him.

For the first time, Nicolas's smooth manner faltered. He sounded sad.

Maybe Lace understood that they were leaving the colt behind, too, because as she pulled the vardo rolling away, the mare's head hung low and she didn't neigh for the baby to follow.

"I'm going to head home, too," Jen said suddenly. She ran toward Silly and, with a few deft moves, she tightened her cinch and bounded into the saddle.

"Okay?" Jen asked as she rode past.

Who could blame Jen for wanting to ride along? The caravan looked as flashy and fun as a circus.

"Sure. I'll see you Tuesday," Sam said, but she couldn't help jogging after them. "I'll be right back," she called to Brynna, but her stepmother was still talking with Norman White.

Witch flattened her ears at the sound of Sam's footsteps coming up behind her. Jake looked over his shoulder at Sam, but he didn't say a word before turning his eyes on Nicolas.

What was Jake thinking? Sam wondered. That she had to say good-bye to Nicolas?

That was true, Sam thought as she caught up with the vardo, but good-bye wasn't what she said first.

"Hey," she puffed.

Nicolas smiled. "Please, thank everyone else for their hospitality. In my rush to leave, I seem to have forgotten my manners."

"Sure," Sam said. Fighting not to pant as she spoke, she asked, "What's going on with Norman, do you think? All this fuss, and now he's just letting you go."

Nicolas gave a wry smile. "You're too trusting, Sam."

"Not about him," Sam began.

"Even though he's got what he wants right there in your round pen, if my instincts are right, he'll keep after me."

"You think so?" Sam said.

Nicolas shrugged. "Just wait and see."

Chapter Fourteen &

The small caravan moved on without her.

Sam turned to walk back to the ranch yard. Her heart ached at each pleading neigh coming from the round pen. The orphan colt already missed Lace.

That is too sad, Sam thought as she walked back toward Brynna and Norman. Dad had joined them, too, but Sam was wondering if Dark Sunshine would allow the little dun into her pasture to play with Tempest, and she wondered how much worse Tempest's cries would be when she was separated from her mother.

"I think we did the right thing," Brynna was saying as Sam approached.

When Norman didn't answer or nod in agreement,

Dad added, "Kid didn't act like he was hiding any-thing."

"It's the sheriff's call," Norman said.

"The sheriff?" Brynna's words were slow with disbelief, and they echoed Sam's reaction.

"When I spoke with him, Sheriff Ballard appar-ently had had several calls about a suspicious drifter in the area . . ."

No way, Sam thought. *Norman is making this up!* They hadn't encountered anyone except Linc Slocum on their ride to the River Bend Ranch. And, big as he was, the rich rancher didn't constitute "several" people. Although, she guessed it was possible Linc had called the sheriff more than once.

"He's not a drifter," Sam said, trying to stay polite for the sake of Brynna's job. "He—"

"Have a little crush on him, do you?" Norman gave an oily chuckle, and followed it with a knowing wink. "I've heard bad boys appeal to some girls, but the sheriff won't be so taken in. He'll stop the boy before he gets too far. Then we'll see what offenses besides horse theft he's hiding in his bag of tricks."

Leaving everyone speechless, Norman White nodded, then returned to his truck. As he drove past, Sam gathered up the courage to ask Brynna what would become of the Spanish Mustang colt.

Before she could, Sam heard galloping hooves approaching.

Sam didn't see Jake touch his black mare, but

Witch slid into a cow horse stop that showered Sam with dust from the hard-packed ranch yard.

What was he doing back already? Why wasn't he riding along with Nicolas and Jen toward Darton?

Jake reined Witch around Sam and sent her at a rapid jog toward Dad and Brynna.

"Somethin's up," Jake said.

No kidding, Sam thought.

"I left the wagon and was ridin' home. Looked back and saw Nicolas gettin' ambushed by Slocum and the sheriff. Looks like Jen is givin' 'em, an earful, but . . ."

"We'll be right there," Brynna said.

"In the truck," Dad insisted.

Sam took a step after them, but Jake halted Witch in front of her, kicked his left boot free of his stirrup, and reached down a hand.

"Sam," Brynna said in a cautious tone.

Riding double on Witch would be as scary as riding a roller-coaster. She'd be plunging headlong into the wind, as fast as she could go, with no control whatsoever.

Sam reached high for the stirrup, set her boot down hard, and grabbed Jake's hand.

"I'll be careful," she said, then she let Jake pull her up.

"Hang on," he said, and Sam barely had time to sling her arms around Jake's waist and suck in a breath before they were off.

Sam closed her eyes against the scenery streaking by. She tried not to feel the sickening swoop as Witch jumped something and the rap against her forehead as Jake's hard black hat brim rocked back to hit her. At last Witch slewed sideways and stopped.

Dust corkscrewed up around them. Sam heard the movement of humans and horses and then her own voice said, "You're a madman. Riding like that could've gotten us killed."

Jake turned in the saddle and looked down into her face.

"Naw," he said, but Sam still felt a little sick to her stomach.

Next, she noticed the cottonwood leaves on the trees around them turning from yellow to orange, yellow to orange, in the glare of strobing red lights on a police car. Then Sam heard Sheriff Ballard talking to Nicolas.

"Son, it would make things a lot easier for everyone if you'd give me permission to search your wagon."

What? Sam leaned to the right, finally releasing her hold on Jake's waist to peer around him and see what was going on.

Why would Sheriff Ballard want to search Nicolas's vardo? The guy couldn't be doing anything wrong. She and Jen had been with him since . . . wow, had it only been yesterday?

Sitting astride Witch, Sam was high enough that she viewed the situation as if it were a play.

Jen was across the clearing, face crimson with anger. Nicolas was beside her, in the driver's seat of the vardo. Though he used the same silky voice he had with Norman White, Jen's palomino was picking up the tension around her and Jen had to work to keep Silly from bolting.

Beneath her, Sam felt Witch exhale hard. Whether from excitement or exertion, Sam couldn't tell, but she knew Jake wouldn't let the black Quarter Horse act up.

"Of course you have my permission to search, Sheriff," Nicolas said. "Just as soon as Mr. Slocum agrees to let you search his house."

Nicolas was being sarcastic, but Sheriff Ballard's expression said a chance to search Linc Slocum's house would be a dream come true.

"I heard him mutterin' in a foreign language," Linc told the sheriff.

Probably no one else heard Jake's disgusted groan, but since Sam sat right behind him, she couldn't miss it.

"Speakin' a different language is no crime," Sheriff Ballard pointed out.

Oh my gosh, Sam thought. Why would Linc try to get Nicolas arrested for being a gypsy? And why would Sheriff Ballard want to search Nicolas's wagon?

Norman White had boasted that the sheriff would stop Nicolas before he got too far, then check to see what offenses besides horse theft he was hiding in his "bag of tricks." Sam guessed that included searching his vardo, but what for?

Sam was leaning to the right, staring past Jake at Nicolas when he asked the same question.

"What exactly is missing, Sheriff?" Nicolas asked, sorting the reins in his hands with such care, there might have been six of them instead of just two. "What would you be searching for? Stolen chickens, laundry off someone's clothesline, missing wallets or crystal balls, perhaps?"

Sam leaned a bit farther right, to catch the sheriff's reaction to Nicolas's sarcasm.

"Of course not," the sheriff said. "I know gypsies aren't all thieves and fortune-tellers."

Nicolas raised an eyebrow.

He was doing it again, Sam thought. First he'd misjudged her and Jen, thinking they were stereotyping him, when they hadn't even known he was a gypsy. Now, he'd sized up Sheriff Ballard's shaggy gray hair and droopy mustache, and decided the small-town lawman was small-minded, too.

Sam wanted to warn Nicolas, but when she leaned even farther to the right, she caught her breath as she started to slip. Jake reached back to stop her fall, and luckily Nicolas didn't need her help.

Although Sheriff Ballard's gaze narrowed for a minute, he understood Nicolas's reaction and explained, "A ring of horse thieves has been operating in this area, and a representative of the Bureau of

Land Management asked me to detain you."

Sam knew it had been Norman White, but Nicolas's glare hit Sam as hard as a slap.

Not me, she thought, then realized Nicolas must think Brynna had notified the sheriff.

Sheriff Ballard had caught the look, too. Realizing Nicolas had come to a faulty conclusion, the sheriff said, "The call was something about a dun colt, but the . . . gentleman who left the message was pretty darn vague."

"I thought you were helping me out, Sheriff," Linc Slocum whined like a second grader. "What with their trespassing and—"

"Norman White was just over at River Bend, talking to Nicolas," Jen began. "He let him go."

Jake inclined his head as if looking down at his mare's hooves, but Sam heard him say, "Tell 'im."

Tell him what? Jake and Jen didn't know Norman had alerted the sheriff to Nicolas after talking to Brynna, but before meeting Nicolas.

But Jake and Jen had been there when Norman had been unable to come up with a reason to keep Nicolas from leaving.

"My dad and Brynna are on their way after us," Sam said. "They were standing right there when Mr. White said Nicolas could leave if the colt stayed behind."

"That so?" Sheriff Ballard asked, but Linc interrupted once more.

"Don't tell me you're the sort of sheriff who won't keep track of drifters! What about homeland security? At least you have to make him explain what kind of jibber-jabber he was talking this morning!"

As if he were completely bored with the proceedings, Nicolas reached into the wagon behind him.

Jake tensed in the saddle before her, but Sam couldn't tell if it was because Sheriff Ballard had straightened, taking offense at Linc's advice, or because Nicolas suddenly twisted around and reached into his wagon.

Should he be doing that? Sam thought it looked kind of suspicious.

If the sheriff hadn't thought Nicolas was innocent, he probably would have told him to stop. But he didn't.

When Nicolas drew out his violin and played "Pop Goes the Weasel," Linc began making a wordless protest.

"Linc sounds like an old car trying to start," Jake muttered.

The sheriff only laughed.

After a few seconds, Nicolas laid the violin across his knees. "Sheriff, I don't know what kind of trouble he's in —"

"Me! Why, kid, if you've got nothing to hide, what are you afraid of?" Linc shouted.

Witch started sideways at the sound and Sam grabbed onto Jake, but he simply rested his hand on the mare's neck and she settled down.

The sheriff tried to do the same with Linc.

"You've said your piece," the sheriff hushed him.

Still mumbling, Linc crossed his arms over his broad belly, leaned back against the front of his champagne-gold Jeep, and glared at Nicolas.

"I apologize for this mix-up," the sheriff told Nicolas, "but as I mentioned, we've had some horse theft around here. I'd like to take a quick look in your wagon; then you can be on your way."

"I'm sorry, too, but you've got no cause to search through my things, and until you do, I'll have to say no," Nicolas said smoothly.

"Hey, I know," Jen said suddenly. She urged Silly forward a few steps and turned the palomino to face Lace and Nicolas. "Just show him your journal. You didn't know you would be stopped, so you'd have no reason to have fabricated any entries, and it tells where you were every day, and you weren't anyplace near here when Shy Boots and Hotspot were stolen!"

"Is that so?" the sheriff asked and his apparent willingness to go along with Jen's genius idea swayed Nicolas from his stubbornness.

"I could do that," Nicolas said, smiling at Jen.

Nicolas said a word to Lace before jumping down from the driver's seat.

It must have meant something like "stay," Sam guessed, because Lace didn't take a step while Nicolas strode to the back of his wagon. When

Sheriff Ballard followed him and Linc crowded close, the mare only swung her heavy head around to watch.

Sam wasn't half so patient. "Go," she hissed at Jake.

With a long-suffering sigh, he rode Witch after the others.

"You know you're just as curious as I am," Sam muttered, but Jake didn't say a word, just guided the mare into place so that they had a good view of what was happening.

Nicolas reached in and grabbed the journal he'd shown Sam and Jen the night before, but when he opened its cover, they all saw a thick pad of dollar bills.

So that's where he kept his money, Sam thought, and she realized he must have hidden it somewhere else when he'd shared his journal with them. That shouldn't hurt her feelings. He'd had no reason to trust them, then.

"Ah ha! Look at that big wad of cash!" Linc crowed. "What are you doing with all this money? Next you're gonna say that gypsies don't believe in banks!"

Jake leaned back against the saddle cantle and shook his head.

"His foolishness still catch you napping sometimes?" Jake asked Sam.

Sam was about to call Linc something worse than

foolish, when Nicolas calmly countered the million-aire's remark.

"That's true for some folks of my great-grand-parents' generation," Nicolas said, "but I have a more practical reason. There's a shortage of ATMs where Lace and I go."

He handed his journal to the sheriff and Sheriff Ballard opened the volume at about its midpoint. Looking down from Witch's back, Sam had just noticed it was written in the sibling code Nicolas had told her and Jen about, when Linc's eyes bulged and he came out with a strangled gasp before sputtering, "W-what's that written in? It's some terrorist language, isn't it?"

Nicolas's single bark of laughter said more clearly than words what he thought of Linc Slocum. Then he turned grinning to the sheriff and confided, "It's shorthand."

Chapter Fifteen ❧

Brynna and Dad drove up as Sheriff Ballard began paging through Nicolas's journal. Spotting them, Linc must have sensed things were about to go even more downhill for him, because he slapped his palms against his legs and edged toward his car.

"I've done what I can of my civic duty, so I'll be—"

"Keep us company a minute more, Linc," Sheriff Ballard said without looking up. Though it was phrased as a request, the sheriff hadn't offered Linc a choice.

Dad climbed out of his new truck and hurried to open the passenger's door for Brynna. He helped her down and for once, she accepted.

When Sam thought what a long, tiring day it had

been for her, she knew it had been even harder for Brynna.

But it was Dad who yawned.

"'Scuse me," he said, covering his mouth. "I was hopin' for a nap after that blue mustang danced me all around the corral this morning, but we've had a little excitement over at our place."

Holding his place in the journal, the sheriff met Dad's eyes and made a vague gesture toward Nicolas.

But Dad shook his head. "Linc shot my dog."

The words seemed suspended in the afternoon air. Lace leaned forward against her harness and the creaking of leather was the only sound.

"I didn't kill no dog," Linc snapped.

"Blaze is alive, but I just finished patching him up," Brynna said.

"That's a mite different from what you told me," Sheriff Ballard said to Linc.

"See here, Sheriff—" Linc began, but then he must have heard the rude jab of his words, because he adjusted them. "I mean, you know what I told you. Coyotes have been all over my property and who knows what they're up to. I did shoot one, but . . ."

Brynna squared her shoulders, and though she still wore her bright blue sundress, Sam saw her stepmother shift into biologist mode.

"What coyotes are 'up to' this time of year, is teaching their pups how to find food so they can live on their own. The pups are small, and it would be pretty surprising if they started out by hunting your half-grown calves. Still, if you do have a problem with coyotes, there are better ways to discourage them."

Linc made a blustering noise, but Brynna didn't let him cut in.

"They don't like loud noises. Car horns, air guns, even yelling works pretty well. And rather than hang their carcasses on your barbed wire, as I hear you may already have done, try marking the edge of your property with simple ammonia. That works much better."

"There's nothing illegal about what I did," Linc insisted. "I'm in the clear on this one."

"Let's get a couple things straight," said Sheriff Ballard. "Coyote hunting is permitted in Nevada. They're not a protected species."

"There, y'see?" Linc gloated.

"That doesn't mean you can discharge a rifle in a congested area or shoot dogs for no good reason," Sheriff finished.

"A congested area!" Linc yelped. "We were out on the godforsaken range!"

"Your definition of 'godforsaken' is mighty peculiar, Linc. By your own admission, there were two juveniles, a minor—you're not twenty-one yet, are you?" he asked Nicolas. "And some pretty valuable livestock within rifle range."

"Lace is a Gypsy Vanner," Jen recited once more. "One of only about a hundred in the entire country."

"So you'll be getting a citation for discharging a weapon in a congested area," he said, then turned toward Dad, "and you'll get one for letting a dog run at large."

Dad's jaw dropped in surprise, but he managed to ask, "There's a leash law?"

"No sir, but your pets have to be under voice control."

"Fair enough," Dad said.

Sam was just thinking how she admired Dad's acceptance of his punishment, compared to Linc's whining, when Linc chuckled. At Dad.

"Now, if you Forsters want to press charges against Mr. Slocum for animal cruelty, you can," the sheriff added.

"But that dog was running with the coyotes! If he'd stuck with his own kind, I wouldn't have mistaken him for one of 'em!"

"Wait. You said you were protecting him from the coyote," Jen said.

"Blaze is black with a white ruff around his neck," Sam added. "He looks nothing like a coyote. We're going to go get his son, so he'll be safe, too."

"Sam," Brynna said quietly, "Sheriff Ballard can handle this."

"You all can tell it to the judge," Sheriff Ballard said. "He might levy fines or lecture the shooter and order him to get some glasses. Now, anyone have questions?"

"Isn't it illegal for them to catch that coydog?" Linc asked.

"Interesting you should bring that up, Linc, because I checked it out after you called me this mornin', and according to NAC 503.140, they don't need a Division of Wildlife license or permit to possess a wolf or coyote hybrid."

After that, Linc gave up and drove home, but the sheriff asked Nicolas if he would delay his trip just one more day.

"Norman White accepted his word on the dun colt," Brynna said carefully.

"That's because Norman sicced me on him," the sheriff snapped.

When he returned the journal, Nicolas took it with both hands and a sigh.

"I wish I could read that." Brynna didn't ask permission, but merely pointed at the journal with a wistful expression. "I'm still charged with finding out what happened to the colt. If I found the herder who saw the colt hanging around his sheep, he might give me some clues."

Nicolas's hands moved over the journal as if he was considering handing it over.

"Mr. Raykov, here's my situation. Clues are what I'm after as well," Sheriff Ballard said. "Sam was instrumental in bringing in Flick—one of the horse rustlers I mentioned—and he's tipped us off to a place we can trap Karl Mannix, another bad one. Now,

Flick doesn't mind rolling over on both Karl and Linc, but he hasn't given me enough evidence to place Slocum under arrest."

"I don't see where I come into this," Nicolas said, "but I'm willing to help."

"I wouldn't smear your reputation or nothin'," the sheriff began.

"Which means you would." Nicolas laughed. He leaned against Lace, threaded his fingers through her black-and-white mane, and worked at a tangle before looking up with a resigned expression. "Still, a little slander this far from home, so my parents won't hear it, probably won't hurt me."

Seeing that Nicolas and the sheriff were about to reach a compromise, Jen swung into Silly's saddle. When Jen glanced toward the sky as if judging the time, Sam reminded herself that Jen had left home three days ago and her family didn't know she was safely off the mountain and back in familiar territory.

"Here's all I want to do," the sheriff said. "Hint, for just twenty-four hours, that you're a 'person of interest' in this horse-rustling case. Then, I sit back and hope Linc will do something stupid."

"I've already blown my schedule," Nicolas said regretfully. "I might as well do a good deed in the process."

Jen wasn't so eager to get home that she didn't have time for another clever idea.

"I know," Jen said, pointing at Nicolas. "When

we were looking at your map, you figured a two-day detour around Darton. If you had a police escort, you could go right through the center of town."

"Brilliant!" Sam said as Jen turned her smile on Sheriff Ballard.

"You got yourself a deal," he said. "We'll call it a contribution to cultural diversity or something like that, shall we?"

Nicolas gave the new plan a thumbs-up in the same instant that Brynna fell asleep. Still standing, she slouched against Dad.

"I've seen a horse do that," Sam whispered, "but never a person."

When her stepmother sagged and her knees buckled, Dad wrapped his arms around her and guided her back to the truck.

Once she was tucked inside, still asleep, Dad turned to Sam.

"It's not easy being Brynna," he said. He stood with one hand on the driver's door of the truck and wore an understanding smile. "She works hard to do everything just right. That's why I'm putting her to bed early and forcing her to sleep late. And woe to whoever wakes her up, got it?"

"I guess you're talking to me," Sam said, and then, since Dad wore such a sweet expression, she added, "Tomorrow's a holiday for me, too, so mostly I'll spend it studying, except first thing in the morning when Jake and I are going to take Blaze out to look for his son."

She held her breath, waiting for something to go wrong. Dad could demand she be sensible or Jake could ask what the heck she was talking about. She crossed the fingers on both of her hands and waited.

"I don't know what we'll do with him once you've brought him back," Dad said, "but I hate to see a young animal suffer if he wants help. You okay with this, Jake?"

Sitting behind Jake, Sam couldn't see his face. Though only a few seconds passed, it took him forever to say, "Sure."

Then, without turning around to face her, just as if they'd discussed the details earlier, he agreed to meet Sam at the river before dawn.

"That's all fine. 'Til then, though, you're coming with me." Dad was talking to her, but he looked pointedly at Witch until Sam threw her leg over the horse's tail and slid to the ground. "You can squeeze in next to Brynna," Dad told her, "and maybe I can save your neck for one more day."

It turned out to be the quietest night Sam remembered since she'd come home to River Bend Ranch.

After supper, Nicolas pulled his vardo up close enough to the barn that he could watch Lace and the dun colt in the big loose box stall.

As a faint drizzle fell, Gram brought Nicolas some Mexican hot chocolate. Sam went with her, then sat near the barn doorway on a bale of fresh straw, petting Blaze as she listened to the hissing rain and the sound of Gram making friends with Nicolas.

"I'm sure you've got all you need out here," Gram said. "But I think hot chocolate's especially nice when it rains."

The muted melodies that Nicolas played on his violin lured horses to the fence of the ten-acre pasture. Nicolas enjoyed Gram's ranch tales as much as the animals liked his music. As Gram told of spring and fall cattle drives, when her parents would load her siblings and cousins into caravan wagons much like his vardo, and take them way up from the ranch and into the little valley, Sam tried to picture Gram as a child. Had girls worn jeans in those days or were they still expected to dress in skirts? Had she worn her long hair in braids or twisted up in a knot as she wore it now?

"What did you do there?" Nicolas asked. He'd stopped playing to sample the cinnamon-spiced cocoa.

"Our buckaroos drove the cattle up in the summer and brought them down in the fall. We were just taken along to frolic beside this glass-clear stream." Gram chuckled. "I suppose it figures that most of all I remember the food! One spring we had a cook, who'd been a Sister of Charity. Don't ask me why she was no longer a nun. I was too young to wonder. But oh what that woman could do to sweet pink beans with wild onions and corn cakes cooked on a big black griddle. She set the men to catching trout at night and didn't waste a single minute between the stream and the frying pan. We wanted to stay up there all summer long," Gram said.

Nicolas took the silent moment to play another song as background to the dreamy look in Gram's eyes.

"Of course, after the rock slide we didn't go there anymore, but my how we missed that spot . . ."

Sam smiled, thinking it would be cool to ride up there with Gram, if only to revive her happy memories. Since Gram had always lived on the ranch, the little valley must be nearby.

Dark Sunshine hung her buckskin head over the fence of the small pasture she shared with Tempest. She'd probably been drawn by Nicolas's violin, but maybe she was listening to Gram's stories, too, thinking of the summer nights she'd spent in a small, happy valley.

"Could you find it again, Gram?" Sam asked. "On one of Brynna's maps?"

"I can't say, Samantha. I haven't thought of that place for years. I remember what it looked like, but not how to get there."

It was dark when Gram stood up, put her hands to the small of her back, and stretched.

"You make sure and tie up that colt tonight," Gram told Nicolas. "See that he doesn't go wandering."

"Oh, he's stuck with us for over a hundred miles," Nicolas said gently. "I don't think anything will make him leave Lace."

Sam sighed. Soon enough, the colt would have no choice.

Sam knew it was time to return to the house, but the rain had moved on and it wasn't a bit cold.

"I envy you your journey, Nicolas," Gram said before she left. "I truly do, and we'll do what we can to see that no one delays you anymore."

"I'll be in in a few minutes," Sam said.

Her body was weary, but her mind spun with random thoughts and she knew she wouldn't sleep right away, so she lingered a bit longer.

Every horse on the ranch stood listening to Nicolas's music, and suddenly Blaze joined in as Nicolas sang of gypsy gold.

When his bow had eased over the strings for one last quivering note, Blaze added a mournful howl and an echo returned to him from the hills.

Chapter Sixteen ❧

Sam couldn't sleep, but she wouldn't let herself look at the clock on her bedside table.

She'd been fretting for hours over Nicolas's departure, not because she'd miss him, but because she couldn't stop thinking of the Phantom's attention to each note floating from Nicolas's voice and violin that night in the forest.

Guilt gnawed at her. Nicolas had a long, dangerous trip ahead, and he was a nice guy, but she was far more worried about the silver stallion.

She tossed onto her right side. Cougar yowled when she rolled against him.

"Sorry, boy," she apologized, but he just thumped his tail on her bed and left her wondering what Nicolas had meant when he said she was too trusting.

Sam turned onto her left side, found a cool spot on her pillow, and closed her eyes, but Cougar hopped up on the side of her body as if he were walking a tightrope between her hip and shoulder. She pushed him off, but the cat padded back up to face her, then patted her cheek with sheathed claws, telling her to stay still.

She blocked thoughts of the Phantom trailing behind Nicolas to Darton, pursuing him through the streets of Reno and beyond. She refused to listen to the whizzing of imaginary cars on freeways or the Phantom's challenging neigh. Would he follow Nicolas anywhere just to hear his song, like the Pied Piper?

That's not going to happen, Sam thought. She flopped onto her back, arms loose at her sides, and tried to match her breaths to Cougar's. It worked to relax her until her eyelids drooped and she saw, all over again, an image of the dead coyote.

Knowing she couldn't let Linc get away with that or injuring Blaze, Sam crept out of bed and went to her desk. She wrote six notes, then nodded in satisfaction. She tiptoed around the house. She didn't exactly hide the notes. It was more like placing Easter eggs so really young children could find them. Still, she knew Dad, Gram, and Brynna would get the point, even though Sam would be long gone, with Jake and Blaze, when they came upon the notes in the morning.

Satisfaction acted like a sleeping spell and Sam nodded off as soon as she crawled back into bed and laid her head on the pillow. Still, she would have slept better if her dreams hadn't been haunted with images of Nicolas skipping across the *playa* in a red scarf and gold earring, sawing at his violin as he was followed by hundreds of prancing horses.

The next time Sam's eyes opened, the clock read 4:33 A.M.

Before the sounds of more tossing and turning could carry down the hall and wake Brynna, Sam edged out of bed. The minute her bare toes touched the floor, she felt better.

Sure, she was an hour and a half too early to meet Jake, but there was always something to do outside. She could check on Lace and the dun colt, kiss Tempest and Sunny on their velvet noses, or stare at the horizon until the first pink light of dawn outlined the Calico Mountains' peaks.

Sam dressed in a gray sweater and yesterday's jeans. Dried jerky, left over from her camping trip with Jen, made a stiff lump in her pocket, but her chest of drawers squeaked, and she didn't want to risk the noise of getting fresh clothes.

Sam picked up her waterproof boots. Just

because it had barely drizzled last night didn't mean the storm predicted for today would be mild.

It was a good thing her slicker was hanging on the front porch instead of here in her room. Its rustle would have awakened Brynna for sure.

Now she only had to worry about waking Blaze, Sam thought as she tiptoed down the stairs, carrying her boots. The Border collie would be alert to the opening of the kitchen door, even though he'd spent the night in the bunkhouse.

Thoughts of the sad dog made Sam hope he did waken when she went outside. It was still dark. She'd like to have him frisking at her heels as she prowled alone around the ranch.

But that would be selfish. The dog's injured side would be tested today as they tracked his coydog son, even though she and Jake had decided to take the truck. She'd let Blaze rest among the cowboys, for now, and only summon him when Jake arrived.

Standing in front of the coats hanging on the front porch, Sam's hand hesitated between her old yellow slicker and the new poncho hanging beside it.

Silver as starshine, the poncho reminded her of the Phantom. Though she hadn't told a soul, that's what had drawn her to the hooded garment in the store. Today she'd be driving out onto the range, into the Phantom's territory. Could there be a better day to wear the silver poncho for the first time?

She pulled it on, settled it over her shoulders, and

arranged it to cover her arms. Looking down, Sam saw it was a perfect match to her braided horsehair bracelet. Then she raised the silver hood and stepped onto the front porch.

Mist tossed through the darkness.

I am a princess knight, wearing a chain mail cloak, Sam thought.

Many people would say she was too old for make-believe, but they were the same people who'd tell her she was dreaming if she insisted she could bid a wild silver stallion to come to her—and sometimes he would.

Sam smiled. Sure, the Phantom only came to her sometimes, but fairy-tale maidens didn't have a 100 percent success record for summoning unicorns, either.

Sam drew a breath of night air. When her bare feet had first touched her bedroom floor, she'd promised herself that she'd go looking for early chores. Now, though, dressed in her silvery poncho, she wanted to walk toward the river.

The minute she stepped off the porch, she spotted Lace nosing the flap of cloth covering the back of Nicolas's vardo. Was something wrong? Sam stared for a minute, waiting, and though she couldn't see the dun colt in the shadows, she had the feeling the Gypsy Vanner mare was only checking on Nicolas as he slept, and the idea made her grin. Sam was glad Nicolas had stayed on an extra day.

Instead of blowing from east to west or north to south, the wind skimmed along the ground, then jetted into sudden updrafts, climbing past her shoulders, past the rooftops, and into the cloud towers that would feed the storm.

Topsy-turvy air currents made her sure the coming storm would be fierce. If Nicolas had been out on the range, he could have crawled into his vardo for shelter, but what about Lace? It would be far better for the big mare to be here at River Bend Ranch, tucked in next to the barn.

Sam looked up into the sky. It seemed beige at first. As she walked past the chicken coop, she decided she was wrong. The sky glowed a pale aquarium green. Thunder rumbled and wind tugged at the hem of her poncho.

Crossing the bridge with quiet footsteps, Sam stared toward the Calico Mountains. She shivered in awe as forked purple lightning stabbed through the clouds.

Sam walked faster as a fine rain began falling.

Squinting against the moisture beaded on her eyelashes, Sam saw the willow trees trailing branches in the La Charla River. A fish jumped, making a small splash. She couldn't see it because of the fog hanging above the river.

At least that's what she thought at first.

She heard another splash and stared so long, her eyes stopped trying to pierce the fog and lifted higher.

There, moving like a shadow in the silver showers, was the Phantom.

My mystical stallion, Sam thought. She celebrated the intuition that had drawn her here until she realized he was waiting for her, on this side of the river.

Fear flashed through Sam, fueled by the lesson of the mother coyote who'd died for coming too close to civilization, but she couldn't pick up a stone and throw it at him. She couldn't shout and break this spell. Once more, the Phantom offered her friendship, and she couldn't bear to scare him away.

Her boots stepped from one patch of dirt to another, avoiding rocks that might crunch or roll, but she needn't have been so careful.

The Phantom trotted her way. He stopped when she did. They stood near enough to touch.

She didn't ask herself what had drawn him to this place at exactly the same time she'd come here. She just tilted her head to look up into the Phantom's eyes and saw him staring down at her.

Old magic, made between them on the day the stallion had been born, flickered from the brown eyes staring through long moonlit strands of his forelock. Sam's veins burned cold-hot at her wrists and temples.

The stallion watched her and love swirled around her heart.

"Zanzibar," she whispered.

His gaze broke away as he circled her at a walk. Pewter dapples shone on his frost-colored coat.

"Did you come to take me across the river?" Sam whispered.

He'd come to meet her, that was for sure, but if they galloped toward the valley as they had before, they'd move into the heart of the storm.

The warning voice in her brain was drowned out by the stallion's nicker, and the soft tread of their footfalls as Sam walked along the riverbank with one hand resting on the stallion's mane.

Before, she'd tried mounting him from a river rock and the sudden change in her height had made him shy away. Vaulting onto his back was dangerous, but everything about a wild stallion was dangerous.

Besides, their friendship had never been based on safety. When she and Jake had first schooled him as a shiny black colt, Jake had told her, "If he wants to strike you, you've had it. He's that fast. It's your job to make sure he never wants to hurt you."

Sam was pretty sure she'd done that part of her job. She'd never hurt the Phantom and he'd always come back to her.

The stallion moved a step past her, so that she was staring at his side. Sam held her breath and picked the places she'd touch.

Softly, she lay her left hand on his withers. When his skin didn't shiver, she knew he understood what came next.

"Take me for a ride, beauty."

Sam vaulted up, landing belly down across his back. Quickly, she swung her right leg over, just above his tail, and then she was astride.

The stallion tossed his head, snorting and prancing.

Don't get too far forward. Don't dangle your feet too close to his flank, she warned herself. Suddenly she was centered. The Phantom felt it the instant she did and he pivoted toward the river.

Cold! Autumn river water splashed up. It didn't feel like the La Charla in the summer, but she didn't have time to think about it. With no stirrups or reins, the only security she had was trust.

Once they reached the other side of the river, she tangled both hands into his mane, then braced herself for the stallion to shake the water from his coat. He did, and she stayed on, and then he moved into a flowing trot.

She should have heard his hooves striking the earth. She should have smelled wet horsehair and felt the sudden fear of cold and darkness and being all alone far from her family and her bed, but she didn't.

She rode in a dream and her thoughts came in far from sensible snatches.

Only along for the ride. Sam had heard that expression before, but when she was astride the Phantom, it was completely true. She didn't guide the great horse. She went where he wanted to take her.

All at once it was too cold to ignore. It wasn't just the breeze blowing past her wet jeans. The wind hitting her face was freezing and the sky had turned sulphur yellow.

To the south, she saw turkey vultures riding the updrafts, and then something hit her cheek. A big raindrop? Another one struck her nose. She dared to take one hand from the stallion's mane and feel for whatever it had been, but she felt only moisture.

Before she could puzzle out what had hit her, more came. The Phantom lifted his knees, prancing over something like snow — no, it was hail.

No big deal, Sam told herself, as popcorn-sized hailstones pelted her hands so fast she couldn't count them.

It happened all the time. It would let up in a minute.

But the vultures that had just been over there were gone.

Hail pounded all around her, bouncing off the back of her poncho even as they bent sagebrush down to the ground.

The hailstones got bigger and the Phantom's trot broke into a lope.

Ow. They were actually starting to hurt now, and she could only hope the stallion didn't try to outrun them.

All at once she couldn't hear anything but the pounding hail. They galloped past a pinion pine tree just as an onslaught of hail stripped a branch loose. As big as her fist and round as softballs, they could kill small birds or animals.

The hail kept hammering down. Sam searched her mind for a place to take shelter, then abandoned the idea. The stallion would know better than she did. And then, as if proving her right, the Phantom bolted into a gait faster than a gallop, faster than a run, and she could do nothing but hide her face against his mane and hope her cold-numbed hands kept their grip.

When the ground tilted up and the stallion deliberately took a meandering path, Sam knew where they were going. The stallion was taking her to the tunnel. Sheltered by stone walls, they'd be safe.

Sam raised her head and opened her eyes just as they entered the tunnel. The stallion only walked a few paces before stopping.

Swathed in darkness, Sam blinked, but she saw nothing.

Outside, the hail sounds turned from pounding, to pinging, to plops. At last, her ears ached in the sudden silence.

Without trying, her breaths matched the Phantom's. Finally they slowed to a normal pace, and Sam realized her hands had stopped holding the silver mane and now clung around the stallion's neck. Although the Phantom's heated body was keeping her warm and she felt incredibly peaceful, Sam worked her interlocked fingers apart, and pushed herself up until she sat straight.

She wanted to thank the Phantom for his friendship, for the ride of her life, for finding shelter and safety, but instinct kept her quiet. Suddenly, she knew why.

Sitting still on the stallion's back in the stone tunnel, she heard something move nearby. Then the growling began.

Chapter Seventeen ❧

Get off. Contented and dazed from her gallop through the storm, Sam resisted orders from the sensible side of her brain. She was afraid to be afoot. Whatever was down there couldn't reach her on the stallion's back. Could it?

There was a stone ceiling just inches overhead. Solid and looming, the rock gave off a cold threat. Sam ducked closer to the stallion's neck, but he was finished cuddling. A hoof rang on rock and he bolted backward until he crashed into a wall. His tail whisked against unseen stone. There wasn't room for a fight.

She had no choice. Wrong—she had choices, but both were bad. She could stay on the Phantom's back until he reared and her head slammed into unconsciousness like it had years ago. Only this time would be different. Jake wasn't beside her. She'd lay in the gloom alone and undiscovered.

Or she could dismount and take her chances with the teeth and claws of an animal that was definitely not glad to see her.

But she might be able to either sprint past the creature or fight back.

Sam slid from the stallion's back. Her legs wobbled. She shivered, and the Phantom picked that moment to rub his cheek against hers, but when she reached up to touch him, her hand moved through empty air.

Her eyes strained, trying to use the bit of light seeping in from outside. The hailstorm had moved on, but a curtain of rain fell across the tunnel's entrance. Sam saw shadows, but that wasn't enough.

Was it a cougar? A bear? Maybe Flick, escaped from prison and hiding here?

Whatever it was had to move again. That would give her clues. She tried not to swallow. Even that small sound could cover a threat.

Waiting, she tried to pinpoint her position. She was pretty sure she was just inside the tunnel leading to the Phantom's secret valley, a few horse lengths from the rust-red and ocher cave paintings of prehistoric horses.

Startling her, the Phantom lowered his head with

a snort of recognition. In the instant before, she heard the thump of a canine tail.

Not a cougar, bear, or bad guy, but a dog. Battling her relief, Sam made out a shape in the shadows just as the stallion and the coydog touched noses.

Blaze's boy, Sam thought crazily. Clearly the two creatures had met, so that growl had been for her. She couldn't blame the coydog. What he knew of humans was horrible.

Blinking, Sam had the impression of gray-black fur over a pale and fuzzy undercoat. Along his spine, a strip of hair rose up like a Mohawk haircut. More fur bristled on the coydog's shoulders.

A sudden lapping sound told Sam the pup had turned his attention from her. His tongue licked the pads on his feet, soothing paws that had traveled a long way. But she must have made some sound, because he stopped and raised his head. Clouds must have parted outside and unmasked the sun, because faint light showed more than the coydog's outline now. His eyes shone amber and Sam's concern for the pup turned back to fear.

Food, Sam thought. Although she knew humans should rarely offer food to wild creatures, the coydog was curled up between her and the way out. Winning him over with food was her best bet.

Feeling the Phantom beside her, Sam tried talking to the pup, even though she knew she wouldn't sound like a member of his pack.

"Yes, I'm going for the jerky in my pocket." Sam's coaxing tone and movement made the coydog's ears prick toward her. "You'll like it. I promise. Then you'll follow me outside and soon your dad will show up with—"

Jake! He would have kept his promise to meet her at the ranch at dawn. And it was getting light outside.

Sensing her uneasiness, the coydog yapped.

"It's okay, baby. I just did something stupid."

How long had Jake waited before banging on the ranch house door? No, he would have waited in Dad's truck with Blaze, then thrown pebbles at her window to wake her. When she hadn't responded, then what?

She couldn't worry about that now. She had to escape the tunnel while the coydog was calm.

Sam flipped an inch-long chunk of jerky toward the pup. He came to his feet before it fell. With a crack of sharp teeth, he caught the jerky in midair and gulped it down.

"You're hungry, aren't you?" Sam asked. She kept her voice relaxed, but this snapping hunger scared her.

The Phantom's shoulder bumped Sam out of the way. Then his head lowered to give the pup a hard nosing.

"Zanzibar, my hero," Sam crooned, suddenly amazed by the scene before her.

She thought of Linc calling Nicolas a gypsy thief. She thought of Nicolas's quirked eyebrow and constant suspicion. Neither of them had half as much reason to distrust each other as the stallion and this coydog.

But these two were getting along.

Even though the pup was a predator who could one day bring down a mustang foal, the Phantom treated the pup as a friend.

The Phantom's nicker filled the tunnel with echoes as he backed away from Sam and the coydog. If a mare's call had beckoned him from the secret valley, Sam hadn't heard it. But something had summoned the stallion. His sleek body bent almost in half and then he turned to go.

Zanzibar? Sam kept the melancholy sound to herself. It was time for him to return to his herd and time for her to try her luck back in the real world. But Sam couldn't help peering after him. She glimpsed his silver waterfall of a tail, but it moved off, fading to a faint haze of gray, before that, too, was erased by the tunnel's darkness.

In a single minute, there was no sight, sound, or smell that indicated the wild horse had ever been there.

But then a whimper as faint as her own breath came from the pup. He'd turned his head to one side. If she could get the coydog outside, Blaze would tell him what to do. If only Jake had brought him.

Then, with solid certainty, she knew that Jake had followed her. Cowboys said Jake could track a bumblebee in a snowstorm. He wouldn't have a moment of trouble following the Phantom's hoof-prints on muddy ground.

Half of Sam hoped the deluge of hail had battered away the stallion's tracks. The other half of her hoped Jake was outside, waiting to help her save this misfit puppy.

Sam walked backward. She dropped bits of jerky and the coydog followed. She didn't take her eyes from him and he watched her just as closely as they emerged into the morning light. And the rain.

Gasping at the sudden chill, Sam pulled up the hood of her poncho, but gusting wind jerked it off again and the pup growled each time she reached for it.

"Fine," she muttered. "I'll leave it down and get pneumonia."

Sam put the toe of one boot behind the heel of the other. If she kept the treeless north face of the hillside across from the mouth of the tunnel, on her right, she should reach the steep downward path in a few minutes.

The rain had to stop soon. Already the light was hazy, as if it had been strained through peach-colored cloth; and though rivulets of rainwater snaked over the dirt, making the path slippery, the thirsty ground would soon soak them up.

"What happens when I run out of jerky?" Sam asked the pup, but that wasn't her worst problem. She couldn't go backward down the hillside covered with shale the size of china plates. It would be safer to turn her back on the coydog and hope he didn't attack.

Sam stopped and stared at the pup. Oversized ears cupped toward her and the coydog yapped his impatience for more food. Sam drew a deep breath, threw him about one-third of her last piece of jerky, then turned around and started down the hillside.

He whined, but he didn't follow. Sam listened between each footstep. Though his cries continued, they didn't come closer.

At least she knew where he was now. And she'd bet he'd return to the tunnel, where he'd made his own den. Besides, if he wanted more easy food, he'd track her.

The thought of tracking made Sam lift her gaze from the trail. She spotted Dad's blue truck. Some distance closer, next to an outcropping of black rock, Jake waited for her in the rain.

Chills covered Sam's arms inside her shirt. For a second, she told herself it was just a reaction to the rain dripping down the neck of her poncho, off her sodden hair, but she knew it was more than that.

Jake had tracked her headlong gallop on the Phantom this far. He could have pursued her the rest of the way to the hidden tunnel and the secret valley of wild horses, but he hadn't. Sam drew a deep breath and held it.

She didn't know what to think. Ever since the accident—no, ever since her return home after the accident—Jake had been protective beyond belief. He'd vowed to stick to her like glue, and he had. But now he stood down there, soaking wet and waiting, instead of barging after her.

What would he say when she reached him? What would she say? It struck Sam that the phrase "Don't ask and don't tell" was perfect for a situation like this.

A scrabble of claws and a panting whine told Sam that the pup was following. When she turned around, he sat, turned his head to one side, and gave a complaining whine.

"Here you go, greedy guts," Sam whispered.

He caught the tossed sliver of jerky, licked his lips, gave a doggish tail wag, and Sam told herself she had no more time to ponder the mysteries of Jake Ely's brain. She had to keep walking, leading this pup toward his new home.

Jake's black oiled cotton duster hung near to the ground and rain dripped off the brim of his black Stetson. He should have looked sinister, but he didn't.

Not to Sam, at least, but the coydog had stopped a few hundred yards behind her to race back and forth, too afraid to come nearer, too hungry to flee.

"Want to get in outta the rain?" Jake asked.

"You mean get in the truck?" Sam asked. "I can't. The coy—"

"I see him. So does Blaze."

Dad's blue truck vibrated with barks and seemed to shift from side to side as Blaze pounced at the windows.

"He's spotted his pup," Sam said.

Jake nodded, but then a blast of wind blew Sam's hood off again.

"Take this, at least, if you won't get inside."

Jake took off his black hat and settled it on her head and for a minute Sam smiled, but then the hat dropped past her ears and blocked her view of everything around.

"It's too big, but thanks." She handed it back, then crossed her fingers, hoping Jake wouldn't ask about the Phantom or her wild ride through the hailstorm. "What if we let him out?"

Jake sighed. "Worth a try," he said, then strode away from Sam to the truck and flung open the door.

Blaze leaped from the truck and hit the ground running. Frantic with joy, the little coydog ran to meet him, letting himself be bowled over before he jumped up and ran circles around his father.

Their joyous reunion continued until Jake took a few steps toward the animals. Then, the coydog froze, lowered his head, and growled. Blaze ran away from the pup, back toward Sam, and the coydog stood barking, unsure if he should obey his wild nature or domesticated one.

All at once, Blaze raced back toward the pup, pinned him, and stood snarling above him.

"What's he doing?" Sam gasped.

"Just showing him who's top dog," Jake said.

And then it became clear the pup wasn't a bit worried. He looked away from Blaze, then closed his eyes and thumped his tail. He looked peaceful, Sam thought, as if he'd come home.

"How should we get him home?" Sam asked.

"Put Blaze in the truck bed with me. I'll rope the young one if I have to, bundle him in a blanket so he doesn't bite me, and haul him that way to River Bend. Then I guess you can pen him up."

"That all makes sense except for the part where the truck won't haul you back to River Bend because you won't be driving," Sam said.

"*You* will," Jake said.

"What? I don't know how to drive! I'm not old enough, I'm —"

"Scared?" Jake asked. He pretended to roll stiffness out of his shoulders, but Sam saw the smile playing on his lips as he watched Blaze and the pup flop down side by side, panting. Jake must be teasing her.

"Big joke," Sam said. "What are we *really* going to do?"

"Got a better plan?"

"You're serious?" Sam asked.

"Leave them be a minute and let me show you. It's easy."

Hands shaking, Sam followed Jake toward the truck, but she wasn't resigned to what he was asking. Not by a long shot.

As Jake pulled open the driver's door, a bit of heat greeted Sam. Okay, that part of driving would be better than riding in the back with the dogs.

Jake climbed into the truck and settled into the driver's seat.

"I can't—" Sam began, and he clamped his hand on her shoulder.

"Stand right here and watch," Jake said.

Sam watched. Starting the truck looked easy. Putting it in neutral—the wiggly middle position—didn't look very hard either, but pushing in the floor pedal to shift into first gear looked like it took some coordination.

"If you grind the gears a little, it doesn't matter," Jake told her. "If you kill the engine—"

"What's that mean? If I kill anything about this truck I might as well run away from home!"

"It's no big deal. Now," Jake said, sliding out of the truck, "just hop up here."

"Why are you so excited about this?" Sam asked.

"Because driving is fun. You'll love it, and you'll always remember I taught you—"

Jake broke off, shaking his head. He seemed embarrassed to have admitted such a thing, and Sam might have gone along with him for that reason alone, except for one thing.

What if she crashed? Suddenly she thought of the car accident that had killed her mother and the morning chill turned icy. Jake and Blaze and the pup would be in the back of the truck without seat belts, without a roof to protect them. If the truck rolled . . .

Sam grabbed the doorframe as Jake nudged her to get into the driver's seat.

"Jake, I can't do it."

"Yeah, you can." Jake lifted her off her feet.

"What are you—?" Sam gasped, and though her fingers released their grip on the doorframe her hands were shaking as Jake deposited her into the driver's seat.

"Hands on the wheel," Jake ordered, but then his voice softened. "I know what you're thinkin'."

"You do?" Sam asked.

"Yep, but you'll be goin' so slow that anything— including a ladybug—can get outta your way. And you'll stop before you get to the bridge over the La Charla."

"Well," Sam began, not at all sure he knew she was thinking about Mom's accident.

Jake looked down at her with the mustang eyes Sam remembered from childhood and said, "I won't let you get hurt this time."

Jake was wrong about what she was thinking, but she couldn't correct him. If he thought she was afraid to drive because she was remembering her accident with the Phantom when he'd been a two-year-old horse, the accident Jake felt responsible for, well, Sam knew she owed it to Jake to do her best.

"I'll give it a try," she surrendered.

"Ride 'em, cowgirl," Jake said, and then he released a buckaroo yell that not only made the hair on the back of Sam's neck stand up, it had both dogs on their feet and barking, too.

Chapter Eighteen ❦

$\mathcal{T}$wenty minutes later, Jake had roped the coydog and bundled him into a blanket.

"I won't hurt him," Jake told Sam.

"I know you won't," Sam said, but she was still amazed at Jake's gentleness.

Cradling the struggling young animal against his chest, Jake climbed into the back of the truck, sat, and wedged his back into a corner against the truck cab, where they'd be most sheltered from the cold wind.

Blaze stood alongside, panting with his ears back, wordlessly begging Jake for mercy.

"Don't you"—Jake grunted; strong as he was, Jake still worked to keep the coydog from thrashing loose—"worry," Jake told the Border collie as Sam prepared to make her first drive with passengers. "You either," he told Sam.

Blaze threw himself down next to Jake and leaned against him. His nearness caused the pup to heave a loud sigh and finally he was still.

With her live cargo settled, Sam braced to do one of the bravest things she'd ever done—drive.

She turned away from Jake, but turned back again when she heard a weird warbling sound.

The coydog shoved his gray-black muzzle out of his blanket cocoon, tilted his mouth skyward, and burst into a long, mournful howl.

What was he doing? Coyotes howled to claim territory, to communicate across long distances, or celebrate a hunt, not like this, not mourning a loss of freedom.

Both Jake and Sam checked Blaze's reaction.

The Border collie pricked his ears forward. Then he laid his head on his front paws. The dog was unconcerned, but Jake closed his eyes and pressed his face against the coydog as if he hated his part in this capture.

Jake cleared his throat. His voice was gruff as he said, "Don't that about break your heart?"

Sam felt as if the entire world had gone still. She'd never seen Jake so touched. He'd be humiliated if he shed a single tear, so she didn't let it happen.

"Naw," Sam said, lifting her chin. "He's singing."

Jake didn't release his hold on the pup as it grumbled, forced its muffled way between Jake and Blaze, then curled up.

"Think so?" Jake asked, unconvinced.

Sam didn't, but she knew the coydog would be safer on the ranch, if only because he was no hunter. In the tunnel, he'd been famished. With winter coming on, he might starve. But she wasn't about to talk to Jake about the tunnel. She stuck with the idea that the pup had been singing.

"Gosh, Jake, I hate it when I know more about Native American stuff than you do. Didn't I read something about a coyote singing the world into being?"

He shrugged and the sleeping pup's head moved on his arm, but his eyes stayed closed. "Grandfather calls coyotes 'song dogs' sometimes, but he makes stuff up when it suits him." Jake cleared his throat once more. "You gonna stand here jawin' all day or you gonna drive?"

The truck gave a terrible screech when Sam turned the key to start it, and found the engine already running, but that was her worst mistake.

Driving home, she killed the engine three times by going too slow. Two out of three times, the ground was so level, the truck just stopped. She caught herself glancing at the window behind her head, but Jake couldn't see her and he didn't make any comments she could hear.

The last time the engine died, though, the truck had almost reached the bridge over the La Charla River. This time, the truck rolled.

The opening that all vehicles passed through to reach the ranch seemed to have shrunk.

"I can't do it," Sam mumbled. Not now, maybe not ever. She stabbed her boot down on the brake and stopped so hard, Blaze started barking.

She turned the key to Off and set the parking brake as she'd seen Dad do. She'd gotten them this far and she was pretty sure Jake could hang on to the pup for the short time it would take him to walk across the bridge and into the tack room, where he planned to sit with Blaze and the pup.

Heart pounding, Sam slipped out of her seat and rushed around to see if everyone in the back of the truck was safe.

All three of them were fine, but if she hadn't hurried she would have missed it.

Brynna would probably call it submissive behavior. Dad would say it didn't amount to much since the critter was half dog, anyway, but as Sam came around to the truck bed, she saw the coydog lick Jake's face.

Grinning so hard it hurt, Sam asked, "If someone with a dog was going away to college, what do you suppose would happen to the dog?"

Jake lifted his shoulder to wipe at the wet spot from the coydog's lick.

"He might live in an apartment that took pets, instead of the dorm. Or, if he had a dog that needed room to run, who says he couldn't set up a permanent camp and still go to class? I've heard some professors bring their own dogs in with 'em."

For Jake, it was a long string of words. And then he added, "Why?"

Sam drew a deep breath and announced, "Happy birthday!"

"I'm—"

She held up a hand against Jake's protest.

He said, "I was just gonna—"

"Hush," Sam interrupted. "It's fair, since I got Cougar from you."

"Sam, I—"

Sam put her hands on her hips. She didn't yell, because the little black spots of the coydog's eyebrows were raised and worried looking, but she leaned forward until she was practically nose to nose with Jake.

Couldn't Jake see that the half wild dog would get more understanding from him, a guy who'd lived his whole life on the range, than from anyone else?

"It's a match made in heaven," she whispered. Jake managed to get in a single word.

"Singer," he said.

"What?"

Jake settled back, holding the coydog securely. "I'm gonna call him Singer."

* * *

If the day had stopped there, Sam thought later, it would have been perfect.

She'd ridden the Phantom, saved Singer, and driven—pretty well—for the first time in her life. Nevada Day would have been a great celebration.

But the day didn't stop there.

She and Jake crossed the bridge with Singer squirming in Jake's arms, trying to see and sniff everything, and jump down to join Blaze as he paced beside them. Then the Border collie streaked away, barking, at the sight of Dad, Pepper, Ross, and Dallas mounted up and riding out, looking like an Old West posse.

Brynna stood on the front porch, but she walked to meet Sam and Jake.

"What's up with them?" Sam asked, looking after the mounted men. But then she noticed Brynna wore her BLM uniform even though today was a holiday. "And why are you dressed for work?"

"I've got some official business to tend to," Brynna answered. "Sam, I'm afraid we misjudged Nicolas. He's gone and he took the colt."

Sam felt the smile melt from her lips. Her head jerked aside to stare at the barn. The brightly painted vardo was still parked beside it.

"His vardo's still here," she pointed out. "He wouldn't have left that behind."

"He did, though," Brynna said.

"No," Sam shook her head. "Uh-uh. He was here when I got up this morning."

"Are you sure?" Brynna asked. "Did you see him?"

"Not exactly," Sam admitted, "but I saw Lace looking in the back of the wagon."

"Lace is gone, too," Brynna said. "Wyatt thinks Nicolas left during the hailstorm, using it as a diversion."

It was possible, Sam thought. The hailstorm had started after she'd ridden away on the Phantom. But the accusation just felt wrong.

"His grandfather gave him that vardo. They worked on it together."

"Maybe he thinks a Spanish Mustang is more valuable," Brynna suggested, but her tone was uncertain.

Sam shook her head. "I just can't believe it."

"I'm pretty surprised myself." Brynna's short, bitter laugh reminded Sam of her stepmother's conversation with Norman White yesterday.

He'd implied she had some stake in the colt's disappearance. He'd wanted to take the foal back to Willow Springs immediately, but he'd let Brynna talk him out of it and asked if she'd stake her reputation and the reputation of the ranch on Nicolas's honesty.

She had.

Now, Nicolas had vanished.

"I've already notified Sheriff Ballard," Brynna told Sam.

"I guess you had to," Sam said. "And Norman?"

Brynna opened her lips and shook her head. "Not yet. I'm still hoping we're wrong."

A sigh built up in Sam's chest. How often had Brynna told her to think with her head instead of her heart? To trust experience, not hope? Her level-headed stepmother must be terribly worried if she was ignoring her own advice.

While Sam pondered what had made Nicolas leave without a word to anyone, Brynna and Jake talked about Singer and tracking Nicolas. Sam refocused on their conversation as they decided there was no sense in Jake joining the search.

"It's going to be an easy tracking job. A draft horse and foal in the mud." Brynna raised her hands in disbelief. "I don't know what he was thinking."

"Not that he could sneak off." Jake shouted the words as Blaze barked, demanding that Jake put his son down even though the pup was dozing in Jake's arm. "I could still go."

Brynna waved Jake away and finally he and the dogs headed for the warm tack room in the barn. Sam gazed after them, satisfied, but when she turned back to Brynna, her stepmother's whole face drooped in despair.

"There's something else going on here," Sam insisted.

"I'm afraid this is one crime we can't blame on Linc Slocum," Brynna told her.

Sam looked down at her boots. She was that predictable.

"Oh—we found your notes," Brynna added with a weak smile.

To Sam, it seemed days, not hours ago, that she'd written notes reminding Dad and Brynna to file a complaint against Linc Slocum for shooting Blaze, then placed them all over the house.

As Sam watched, her stepmother's fingers kneaded the space between her eyebrows. She must be getting a headache. Compared to the federal charges Norman White might file against Brynna and Nicolas, the urgency of taking Linc to court over injuring Blaze probably didn't seem that important.

"It could wait, I guess," Sam said.

"No. The man deserves to be punished. This is something we can prove. As soon as the courthouse opens tomorrow, we plan to follow up," Brynna said. "Believe me, he won't get away with this. At least not easily."

Pulling her car keys from her pocket, Brynna stared at the white BLM truck as if she couldn't stand the thought of pursuing Nicolas.

Sam toyed with the idea of announcing that Jake had taught her to drive, but she kept quiet. This might not be the best time for another surprise.

"Come with me," Brynna invited. "It's not going to be fun, but I might need help with the horses if we come upon Nicolas before your dad and the hands do."

Sam didn't want to go, but she considered the awkwardness brought on by Brynna's pregnancy and agreed. "Okay. Can I just change into something dry, first? It'll only take a minute."

Brynna nodded, and Sam hurried toward the house. As she did, a dark thought invaded her mind. Yesterday, Nicolas had told her she trusted too easily. Maybe he'd been warning her about himself.

Chapter Nineteen ⌒

$\mathcal{S}$am had dressed in dry, warm clothes and she was hanging her silver poncho back on its front porch hook when the phone rang. She grabbed her leather coat with fleece lining and called up the stairs, "I'll get it, Gram."

The minute she heard the voice calling, though, she was sorry she hadn't just walked on out the door.

"That kid cut 'n run, didn't he?" Linc crowed.

"Where'd you hear that?" Sam asked. She'd never get used to the speed with which news spread in a small town, and though stalling would do no good, keeping things from Linc Slocum came naturally to her.

"Sheriff Ballard stopped in at Clara's for coffee to

go, right after he talked with Brynna—boy, I bet her face is red." Linc chuckled. "He gave Clara a 'be on the lookout' warning for that kid and the horses."

"There's more to this," Sam began.

"I just bet there is! I bet he's to blame for all this horse trouble." Linc's voice took on a wheedling tone as he went on. "Don't he look kinda familiar to you, Samantha? Don't he look like a guy you saw hanging around with Karl Mannix?"

He must be joking, Sam thought. Nicolas was exotic-looking and a complete stranger. Hadn't Linc been the one to brand him a drifter?

"Yeah, I'm thinking I saw him in these parts in about May or June, right around the time my Appy colt disappeared."

"I don't think so," Sam said.

"That's because you don't want to believe the truth—" Linc began.

Sam sucked in a breath, tried to put together something polite to say about Linc Slocum lecturing *her* about the truth, but she was still trying to talk while he went on.

"His kind of people, gypsies, move around for a reason," Linc said. "They're always working on a scam. You heard the expression being 'gypped,' right? Well now you know where it came from."

"That's just ridic—"

"The evidence speaks for itself," Linc said smugly.

Sam sighed, once more hearing Nicolas telling

her she was too trusting. She hated the possibility that Linc could be right.

Then, Linc jarred her gloom.

"Tell me, can you, Samantha?"

"Tell you what?"

"Nicolas's last name."

Sam felt the same way she had when she'd killed the truck's engine and her head had hit the back of the seat. The suddenness of Linc's question was all wrong.

Why did he want to know? And why had his tone changed from giddy to serious?

Sam could have told Linc the information was none of his business, but something else Nicolas had said made Sam answer.

"Raykov," Sam said, but she was hearing Nicolas's voice as he quoted Napoleon.

Never interrupt your enemy while he's making a mistake.

The minute she hung up the telephone, Sam's brain chattered another message.

Last night when she'd woken from a dream about Nicolas acting like a Pied Piper for horses, she'd wanted to run to the vardo, wake him, and make him promise not to play his violin until he'd left the Phantom's territory.

Silly? Yes, but now the dream offered her another clue. If Nicolas was gone for good, he would have taken his violin with him.

Sam sprinted out the door and headed straight for

the vardo. Brynna shouted something after her, but she didn't slow down.

Feeling a little like a burglar, she drew back the curtain covering the back of the vardo. Curved wood polished by skilled hands glimmered back at her. She wanted to grab the violin, hold it aloft for Brynna to see, and dance around playing it, but of course she couldn't.

Instead, Sam ran to the BLM truck, slipped into the passenger's seat next to her stepmother, and slammed the door like an exclamation mark before turning to Brynna.

"He left his violin behind," Sam said, then laughed as Brynna held up her right hand, crossed her fingers, then kissed them for luck.

Brynna drove carefully, but she didn't waste any time.

"Now, maybe I can quit kicking myself for calling the people who adopted the other member of the colt's herd," she said without taking her eyes from the road. "First thing I did this morning was let them know I might have a Spanish Mustang stud colt available for adoption."

"That would be so great," Sam said. "If he could be reunited with part of his herd . . ."

"It gets better," Brynna said with a smile. "I don't know if anything will come of it, but some fanciers of the bloodlines are trying to get the horses 'repatriated' to Good Thunder Meadows."

It took Sam a second to puzzle out what Brynna meant.

"Do you mean, they might get taken back home?" Sam asked.

"Stranger things have happened," Brynna said.

Just then they passed the turn-off to Blind Faith Mustang Sanctuary. About a mile ahead, they saw Dallas, Dad, Ross, and Pepper headed toward Cowkiller Caldera.

"Now I know he's not on the run," Sam said as she and Brynna drove past the men and waved. "Nicolas wouldn't head back into the mountains. If he was trying to escape, he'd go toward town."

Brynna nodded, but she was looking through her window, following Lace's tracks in the mud.

"They look like they were made with the bottom of a teakettle," Brynna muttered, and it was a good thing she was driving so slow, following the tracks, because they both spotted the riders at the same time.

"Hey!" Sam said, and Brynna swerved left as Sheriff Ballard, riding his grulla mustang Jinx, rode up out of a ravine on their right.

"Look who's with him," Brynna said as Nicolas, riding Lace bareback, came into sight with the dun colt dancing alongside.

Brynna lowered the truck's window and called out, "I guess everything's all right."

Sheriff Ballard and Nicolas laughed.

"Could hardly be better," the sheriff said.

Sam didn't bother rolling down her window. Despite the cold wind blowing against the car door, she shoved it open and greeted Jinx with an affectionate neck pat, then turned in time to let Lace whuffle her lips over her coat.

"Let me explain," Nicolas said before anyone could ask questions. Shifting on the mare's broad black-and-white back to look at Sam, he said, "Your friend Jennifer is partly to blame."

"Jen?" Sam gasped.

"And her turkey vultures." Nicolas gave a nod. "Lace woke me when the colt wandered off this morning, and I saw circling turkey vultures."

Sam shuddered. She knew the birds were misunderstood, but they did eat dead things. And the colt had been missing. Sam knew why Nicolas had flung himself on Lace's back and galloped away from River Bend Ranch without leaving a note or telling anyone where he'd gone. She would have done exactly the same thing.

"But he was all right," Brynna said. For a second, she and the others glanced at Sheriff Ballard as he took a two-way radio from his saddle and reined Jinx aside to talk, but then Brynna studied every inch of the little dun mustang.

"By the time I reached the place where I thought they'd been circling, they were gone," Nicolas said.

"The storm," Sam said as she remembered seeing

turkey vultures, too. They'd vanished just before the sky cracked open and pelted her with hail.

"Right, and though Lace had no trouble finding him—without vulture navigation," Nicolas joked, "you cannot imagine what it's like to give a horse its head and expect it to carry you through such a violent storm to safety."

Sam bit the inside of her cheek to keep from laughing. She had a pretty good idea of how Nicolas had felt, and when he leaned down and hugged Lace's neck, she felt a tug of longing for the Phantom.

"So, everything's all right." Brynna sighed.

"You keep saying that." Sam laughed, but as she realized how much Brynna had agonized over this, she understood.

"Actually," Sheriff Ballard said, rejoining them, "everything's better than all right, and though I don't want to count my chickens before they hatch, I think I may have Sam to thank for something real big, real soon."

"Me?" Sam said, but her incredulity shattered as she thought of her phone conversation with Linc. "Linc Slocum's done something else stupid, something having to do with Nicolas, right?"

Excitement blazed through Sam and when the sheriff nodded, she imagined an explosion of triumphant fireworks.

"Tell me!" Sam begged.

"Well, I've been talking to Linc off and on since

yesterday, kinda leavin' the door open for him to come up with something," he drawled.

"And he did," Sam filled in.

"He just faxed a document in to my office, says it's evidence that 'speaks for itself,' but it turns out that this 'communication' between Karl Mannix and Nicolas, here, is something we confiscated from the computer in Mannix's cabin last spring."

"He gave you the same thing?" Brynna asked.

"We held it as evidence against Mannix, but we've been trying to find out if it was ever sent. And to whom."

"Now I guess you know!" Sam crowed. "And the note Linc gave you was exactly the same?"

"Well, it did have one minor change," Sheriff Ballard said. "This note was directed to Nicolas Raykov."

"I'm confused," Nicolas said. "I don't remember telling him my name."

"You didn't. I did," Sam said. She clapped her hands in delight, though she really felt like dancing.

"I'll pick him up for falsifying evidence," Sheriff Ballard went on, "and then, I think I'll have enough for a search warrant. Not that I expect to find anything."

"Why not?" Nicolas asked. "It sounds like he's a fool."

"He just panicked, and saw you as a target of opportunity," the sheriff said. "Just like we hoped."

"Glad to be of service," Nicolas said, making as much of a bow as he could from Lace's back.

The sarcasm drained from his face then, and his left eyebrow was no longer raised in skepticism as he slid down from Lace and walked over to Sam.

"I have to thank you for something."

"Okay," Sam said carefully, but she wasn't prepared for Nicolas to pick up both of her hands as he faced her.

"Remember me saying you were too trusting?" he asked.

"Sure. I was thinking about it this morning," Sam answered.

"I bet you were," Nicolas said, glancing at the colt. "But as it turns out, I was wrong. You trusted me when others didn't, and you stood up for me, and I thank you."

Feeling the flush on her cheeks, Sam shrugged, but Nicolas still held on to her hands.

"Perhaps your friend Jennifer would say you were like her turkey vultures," Nicolas teased. "You took something poisonous like Linc Slocum's judgment of me, and not only did you make the poison go away, you turned it into something good."

"I'll say," Sheriff Ballard told her.

Grateful, but more embarrassed than she remembered being in her life, Sam covered her blushing face with her hands.

In the brief darkness, she saw the Phantom again, leaning over Singer, grazing a growling pup with gentle lips.

Sam sighed. If it was true that she had a touch for turning bad things good, she wasn't the only one.

From
Phantom Stallion
∞ 24 ∞
RUN AWAY HOME

Cold desert winds spun snow dust off the ground and into a white whirlwind that surrounded Samantha Forster and the bay mustang she rode. She pulled her fleece-lined coat up to her chin. The huge stone barn at Three Ponies Ranch had just come into view, and she aimed her horse for it.

Sam glanced at her watch. She wasn't late, but she hadn't passed any of the Ely brothers hurrying off to work. She didn't hear doors slamming, buckets clanking, or truck engines warming up in the thirty-degree morning. The ranch ahead lay oddly silent.

Sam hurried Ace out of his walk and into a jog as they passed Three Ponies' front pasture. For a second, the bay threw his head high and she heard him suck in the scent of frosty sagebrush. Then, the second stirring of her legs, or the December wind whooshing his tail forward to tickle his flanks, made Ace dance.

Hooves churning, the bay insisted he should break into a lope.

"Save it," Sam told her horse.

And when a stocky chocolate-colored gelding galloped toward them, then raced along his pasture fence and she *still* didn't let Ace break out of a jog, her bay mustang gave a little buck just to show Sam who was boss.

"Not you," she corrected him, but she settled more firmly into her saddle, just in case.

They were in the Elys' ranch yard now, and though Sam considered herself a good sport, there was no way she wanted to start the morning with a surprise rodeo performance for the Ely brothers and their parents.

"Awful quiet," Sam said to Ace as they passed five white hens digging in their toenails for better traction as they raced for their coop.

The flock was the only sign of life, though her friend Jake should have had his mare Witch loaded in a horse trailer, ready to go. Sam had expected Jake to be leaning against the trailer, arms crossed with his Stetson tipped over his eyes, waiting impatiently for her to get here.

Scanning the ranch yard once more, Sam spotted

Gal, the Elys' German shepherd, digging at the bottom of the barn door.

Of course, Sam thought, smiling. Jake must be inside. She'd bet he hadn't been able to resist a few more minutes of play with Singer, his coydog pup.

She didn't blame him. After all, Singer was the reason Sam had ridden over to Three Ponies Ranch instead of waiting for Jake to pick her up on his way to Willow Springs Wild Horse Center.

Sam heard the empty porch swing creak as the wind pushed it to the limit of its chains. And then a door slammed. Twisting in her saddle, Sam saw she was wrong about Jake. He wasn't in the barn, because here he came.

Wide-shouldered and purposeful, Jake strode toward her.

Sensing her distraction, Ace snorted, turned to face Jake, and Sam let him. Her mouth had already opened on a greeting when Jake jerked his black Stetson toward the hitching rack in a wordless sign that she should tie Ace and dismount.

From someone else, the gesture might have been rude, but not from Jake. Western movie characters who were "strong, silent types" could easily have been based on cowboys like him.

As Sam slung Ace's reins over the hitching rail, Jake came to stand beside her.

"Good morning," she said. "It's almost Christmas."

Sam knew she could wait all day for Jake to join

her excitement. After all, she hadn't asked him a question, had she?

Sam bent, loosened Ace's cinch, and heard her horse groan with relief. Just when she was thinking her horse was a better communicator than Jake, he spoke up.

"You're just in time to welcome back everybody's hero."

Sam straightened to face Jake.

"Huh?" she asked, rubbing her chilled hands together.

"Kit's coming home today," he said.

"Kit?" Sam gasped. "Really?"

Kit was the oldest of the six Ely brothers, the one she barely remembered. He'd left to follow the rodeo circuit just after graduating from high school. Though he rarely came home, most folks in the area followed Kit's career.

Last summer, it had been big news when Bryan Ely had mentioned Kit's purchase of a new red truck with his rodeo winnings. Before that, Clara had taped a clipping from "Rodeo Today" to her coffee shop cash register because it showed Kit Ely riding a blue roan bucking horse named No-No Nitro.

If the rumors Sam had heard were true, Kit was headed for the national finals in bronc riding.

Jake was right. Kit was definitely a local hero.

"Wow, you mean he's home for Christmas?" Sam asked.

"He will be," Jake said. "He called at about midnight. Don't know if Mom even slept. She was up before daylight makin' cinnamon rolls. Adam called in and took the day off from his kayak guide job in Reno. Bryan and Quinn are waitin' to go out and evict that deer herd from the timothy hay field." Jake shook his head over his brothers. "Dad's goin' in late to work and even Nate stayed home, and he's got some big paper due that he was gonna go in and research at the library."

As Jake glanced back at the river rock ranch house, Sam figured six of the eight members of the Ely family were probably sitting around the kitchen table, out of the icy winds.

"You want to go back in?" Sam asked, in case Jake had left the rest of his family to come meet her.

"No, but Mom'll wring my neck if I leave before Kit gets here. So, you might as well give Singer some time while I work the kinks out of Witch. You mind?"

"Of course not," Sam said.

She looked after Jake as he went to catch his mare, Witch. Maybe it was just the squabble with his mother that was keeping Jake outside, but Sam didn't think so. And there was something else she wanted to ask him.

It seemed like she'd heard the championship rodeo was nicknamed "Cowboy Christmas," because contestants could win huge prizes. Wasn't it held about now? Eight hundred miles away in Las Vegas?

So why would Kit be coming home, now?

Sam didn't ask. She didn't try to get Jake to explain what was bothering him, either. Jake had been her friend since they were little kids and though he was more comfortable with horses than people, over the years she'd learned to read his silences pretty well.

If she stayed alert, she'd figure out what it was about Kit's return that made Jake act annoyed instead of excited.

The Elys' dog Gal was still whining when Sam reached the barn. The dog butted her nose at the space where the barn doors rattled against their bolts as the wind fought to snatch them open.

Sam laughed at the dog's determination as Gal tried to squeeze 130 pounds of German shepherd through a slot barely wide enough for a mouse.

But Sam knew why Gal was trying so hard. Singer, Jake's coydog, was making high-pitched yaps, begging the big dog to come play.

The pup was irresistible to Sam, too. Because of Singer, she'd been to Three Ponies Ranch more in the past three weeks than she had in the last two years. She adored her dog Blaze's half-wild pup, but it hadn't been hard to give him up. From the moment she'd seen Singer mirrored in Jake's eyes, she'd known the two belonged together.

Not that it was easy raising a little creature with warring natures.

Jake insisted the coydog had to socialize with outsiders to his Three Ponies territory, so he'd had Sam work with the pup as much as she could.

"And I feel like a real outsider today," Sam muttered to Gal as she worked to loosen the barn door bolt. "I don't belong in the middle of a family reunion."

The German shepherd gazed up at Sam with confused eyes, then pawed with renewed energy at the base of the doors.

"Okay, okay," Sam told the dog.

The bolt slid free. As Sam eased inside, she almost tripped over Gal.

By the time Sam closed the door behind them so that Singer couldn't escape, the dogs had bowed in tail-wagging greeting to each other.

"You lucky dog," Sam told Singer as he bounced away from Gal and jumped high enough to lick Sam's nose. "It's warmer in here than it is in my bedroom!"

Three Ponies Ranch had been a cavalry post during the Civil War, and the main house, barn, and a small structure the Elys called "the little house" were built with walls that were two feet thick to withstand attack by hostile Indians.

And that, Sam thought, smiling, was kind of ironic, since Jake's dad Luke was a full-blooded Shoshone.

Singer and Gal didn't care about any of that, as they raced around the barn in crazy circles. Openmouthed and agile, Singer bounded over hay bales, then ran with his head low enough to snap at Gal's paws. When the big dog swung around to face him, Singer gave a surprised bark. But he darted aside, easily dodging Gal's playful charge.

While the dogs played, Sam took Singer's light leather harness from a nail. Singer had slipped his head through every collar that wasn't tight enough to choke him, and he couldn't be trusted to stay nearby on his own, so the harness and long leash was a compromise to keep him safe. After all, his mother had been shot for venturing too close to civilization.

When Singer's gray-brown ears caught the jingle of a buckle on the harness, the coydog stopped. Panting and alert, he trotted away from Gal and bumped against Sam's legs.

Gal threw herself belly down in the straw, watching as the pup ducked his head into the harness and Sam clicked the buckles closed around his body.

"Good boy," Sam said, rubbing her hands all over the pup.

Singer laid his ears back and made a worried sound, but he knew this was the price he paid for time outside, and Jake had convinced Sam that constant handling would help Singer listen to his tame nature instead of his wild one.

"Let's go," Sam said, shouldering the barn door open.

Singer gave Gal a single backward glance before following Sam into the wind, but they'd only run a few steps when the pup stopped to watch his master.

Jake had brought the blue Scout truck, which he shared with his brothers, into the middle of the ranch yard. He'd loaded Ace into the horse trailer and now, loose in the saddle, Jake showed the ease of a lifelong horseman as he rode out his black mare's irritation.

Jake squinted at a flapping roof shingle that the winds had peeled up on the bunkhouse while his heels and hands dealt with Witch's fuss.

Sam hunched her shoulders inside her jacket. This morning, the thermometer on her front porch at River Bend Ranch had stayed stubbornly below freezing when Sam thumped it. Winds like these usually blew in late afternoon. Jake's horse, Witch, seemed to know it.

Jake turned the horse's tail to the gusts and waited for her to hump up her back and buck.

While Sam had done all she could to keep Ace from bucking this morning, Jake seemed eager for it. But Witch didn't look serious about pitching Jake off her back. She just seemed grouchy either because Jake had hurried her through breakfast or because she'd spotted the horse trailer with Ace already inside and figured, rightly, that it was waiting for her.

Hands easy on the reins, Jake swayed with Witch's movements. Tilting his chin toward his chest, Jake coaxed the mare into loping figure eights. His hair was finally growing out, and Sam saw the ends of it gleaming blue-black beneath his Stetson.

The wind's sudden blast broke Singer's concentration. He wrapped the leash around Sam's knees and gave a bunch of excited yaps. While she settled him down, Sam thought she heard something.

Could it be Kit?

Over the wind's screech, Sam listened for an approaching truck. She kind of wished Kit would hurry.

But it wasn't an engine's roar that soared above the wind. There was a sudden crack. A branch snapped off a cottonwood tree as if a giant hand had swatted it down.

Ace's hooves drummed inside the horse trailer and Witch shied. Jake ducked as the branch blew past, but it was still airborne, bobbing as if it were carried by an invisible wave, when Jake wheeled Witch toward the naked branch, making her face what she feared.

But the branch didn't hit the ground. It struck the windshield of Jake's truck and broke it.

Like silent lightning, a zigzag crazed the glass.

Singer cringed at the sound, then stood barking.

"Shh," Sam said, petting the pup into silence.

Suddenly, as if she had to show up the misbehaving pup, Witch gave a sigh and stood calmly. As soon as Jake cued her to approach the horse trailer, she did it.

Jake's right boot had lifted from his stirrup and nearly cleared Witch's back when the mare shied again, hard enough that Sam actually heard Jake's teeth crack together.

"Oops," Sam said, but then Gal rushed up beside her and Singer lunged to the end of the leash.

Light-bodied but quick, he didn't manage to jerk the leash from Sam's hand, but his leap surprised her.

All three animals had sensed something, and this time it wasn't the wind.

Sam glanced at Jake to see what he thought, but his attention was focused on Witch. His leg came on over the mare's back and he stayed balanced on his left stirrup.

Only after he planted both boots on the ground did Jake stare in the direction in which the mare's ears pointed.

Through a thin veil of blowing snow, Sam made out a stranger coming down the road. He had a saddle balanced on one shoulder and the fringe on his leather chinks flapped out like raven's wings.

With a single woof, Gal bounded out of the barn, past Sam and Singer, and stopped next to Jake.

The dog leaned against his leg before she raised her black nose. Sniffing, she searched the wind for more than sagebrush and horses for a full minute before her tail curled over her back, wagging.

"It must be someone she knows," Sam told Singer when the pup whined.

As Gal catapulted toward the front gate, barking,

the ranch house door slammed open. Maxine and Luke Ely, Nate, Adam, Quinn, and Bryan all came out smiling.

"Kit," Jake said to himself.

Read all the Phantom Stallion Books!

#1: The Wild One
Pb 0-06-441085-4

#2: Mustang Moon
Pb 0-06-441086-2

#3: Dark Sunshine
Pb 0-06-441087-0

#4: The Renegade
Pb 0-06-441088-9

#5: Free Again
Pb 0-06-441089-7

#6: The Challenger
Pb 0-06-441090-0

#7: Desert Dancer
Pb 0-06-053725-6

#8: Golden Ghost
Pb 0-06-053726-4

#9: Gift Horse
Pb 0-06-056157-2

#10: Red Feather Filly
Pb 0-06-056158-0

#11: Untamed
Pb 0-06-056159-9

#12: Rain Dance
Pb 0-06-058313-4

#13: Heartbreak Bronco
Pb 0-06-058314-2

#14: Moonrise
Pb 0-06-058315-0

#15: Kidnapped Colt
Pb 0-06-058316-9

#16: The Wildest Heart
Pb 0-06-058317-7

#17: Mountain Mare
Pb 0-06-075845-7

#18: Firefly
Pb 0-06-075846-5

#19: Secret Star
Pb 0-06-075847-3

#20: Blue Wings
Pb 0-06-075848-1

#21: Dawn Runner
Pb 0-06-081538-8

#22: Wild Honey
Pb 0-06-081539-6

HarperCollins*Children'sBooks*

www.harpercollinschildrens.com